Alfreda Ab

If you want my opinion, I think it's
quite astonishing that in this day
and age such a mix-up could take
place. That two people as different as
Norbert and Alfreda could end up
with each other's voices is nothing
short of a scandal.

JEROME FLETCHER

illustrated by Sue Heap

Alfreda Abbot's lost voice

MAMMOTH

First published in Great Britain 1988
by Oxford University Press
Published 1990 by Mammoth
an imprint of Mandarin paperbacks
Michelin House, 81 Fulham Road, London SW3 6RB

Mandarin is an imprint of the Octopus Publishing Group

Text © Jerome Fletcher 1988
Illustrations © Sue Heap 1988

ISBN 0 7497 0037 8

A CIP catalogue record for this title
is available from the British Library

Printed in Great Britain
by Cox & Wyman Ltd, Reading

In memoriam.
Anne and Felix Fletcher

I missed my vocation in life.
I should have been a child.
L.D.

Chapter 1

It was about this time that the weather took a turn for the worse. In the main it had been cold, but dry. Now the temperature rose a little and the rain came down. People hurried to and fro with collars turned up or hunched under umbrellas. During the day the rain made the pavements and puddles silver-grey and at night, under the glow of the yellow street lights, they turned to dull gold. The air became dank and humid. This is precisely the sort of weather that germs enjoy most. So, rather than remaining hidden, they began to appear in public, lurking in the fog, hanging around at street corners, looking to make a nuisance of themselves, intent on making somebody's life a misery.

Their first aim is always to find some premises where they can create a rumpus and generally have a good time. This usually means picking on some poor, weakened individual. Often it's someone who hasn't wrapped up warm enough. Perhaps they had gone out without a hat or a scarf. Anyway, having found a suitable victim, the germs move in. On this occasion one of their victims was Alfreda Abbot.

The first thing Alfreda knew about it she was being kept awake at night with a thumping headache as the germs started shoving the furniture around upstairs and hammering in nails to hang their pictures on. Her mother gave her some aspirin to try and get rid of them, but this had little success. They simply moved down to her throat and started redecorating. This involved stripping off all the old paint and wallpaper with wire brushes, blow-torches and scrapers (at least, this was what it felt like to Alfreda!) and the dust that all this redecorating raised made her sneeze violently.

When the redecorating was finished, the germs moved down to her chest and decided to hold a party. They invited a whole lot of friends round, which caused all sorts of congestion. The atmosphere became thick and smoky, and this made Alfreda cough incessantly. Even after several days the party was still going strong. But there was worse to come.

Alfreda arrived home from school one day in this sorry state of ill-health and flopped into a chair at the kitchen table. Marjorie, her mother, made her a cup of tea and put it down in front of her. Alfreda said nothing. Marjorie stood with her arms folded waiting for a response.

'It doesn't cost anything to say thank you!' she said. Alfreda opened her mouth and pointed at it with her finger. This did nothing to improve her mother's humour.

'Please, Alfreda. No silly games. If you're hungry, you ask properly. I'm in no mood for charades.'

Still Alfreda said nothing. Instead she reached down into her bag and took out an exercise book and pencil. She wrote something on a piece of paper and handed it to her mother. This is what it said:

Mrs Abbot tutted and shook her head.

'Honestly, you're so careless! Why can't you look after your things better? Where did you lose it?'

No sooner had she asked this question than Marjorie realised there was little point in asking it because Alfreda couldn't answer it even if she knew the answer. She tried again:

'Did you have it at school?'

Alfreda thought for a moment, then nodded.

'You must have lost it coming home. Probably on the bus. Well, you'd better hope someone has found it and handed it in, otherwise there'll be all sorts of problems. We'll have to wait till George gets home. He can drive you to the Lost Voice Office and see if it's there.'

Alfreda put her elbow on the table and rested her head in her hand. Her mother's mood softened when she saw how miserable Alfreda was looking. Perhaps she could have been a little more sympathetic.

'Never mind,' she said. 'Don't worry. It'll turn up. Drink your tea.' And Marjorie went out to make some toast.

At that moment Reg appeared looking rather pleased with himself. The small lump of mud stuck to the end of his nose betrayed the fact that he'd been out burying a bone somewhere. He stood and looked at Alfreda who looked back at him and said nothing.

'What's the matter with you?' he asked. 'Cat got your tongue?'

Alfreda pulled a face at him and showed him the piece of paper she had shown her mother. Reg screwed up his eyes and scanned the piece of paper for quite some time. Not that there was anything wrong with his reading. It's just that, being a dog advanced in years, his eye-sight was not as good as it used to be.

'That's bad luck,' he said finally and with genuine concern. 'Still, if the worst comes to the worst you can always borrow mine.'

Alfreda gave him a look that seemed to say 'Thanks, but no, thanks.' After all, who wants to go around sounding like a dog?

ome time later, George Abbot arrived home from work and was greeted with the news about his daughter's lost voice.

'That's a blessing,' he said. 'Perhaps we'll get a little peace around here at last!'

'George, that's unkind. Alfreda's very upset. You'll have to take her to the Lost Voice Office and see if it's been handed in.'

George made the point that the office would be closed at this hour.

'No it isn't. It stays open until ten o'clock.'

'Can't it wait till tomorrow?' he said. 'Or better still, some time next year?'

From the way Alfreda scowled at her father you could tell she didn't think that last comment was very funny.

'Besides, I haven't had any supper yet,' he complained.

'The sooner you leave, the quicker you'll be back.' And Marjorie turned him round and pushed him towards the front door.

George realised that he wasn't going to win this argument and resigned himself to his task.

'Come on then,' he said to his daughter.

'You'll need her birth certificate,' said Marjorie, hurrying off to fetch it.

Alfreda and her father drove into the centre of town and after George had parked the car, the two of them walked the short distance to the Town Hall. This was a massive, ornately decorated building. The front of the edifice consisted of a row of tall pillars with fluted columns and carved capitals, such that the Town Hall resembled nothing so much as an ancient temple. Once inside, George asked a man dressed in uniform if he could direct him to the Lost Voice Office.

'Up the stairs to your right. You'll have a wait, mind. There's a crowd of people. Always the same when the fog comes down!'

George thanked the man and he and Alfreda made their way up the wide, stone staircase. A dark red carpet ran up the middle and was held in place by brass stair-rods. Where the staircase forked left and right Alfreda and her father turned right and when they got to the top they saw in front of them, through an elaborate arch, the entrance to the Lost Voice Office.

'He wasn't joking,' said George when he saw the number of people in the room. Numbered wooden seats were set out in rows and nearly every available one was taken. Father and daughter found two vacant ones near the back and sat down. An eerie, unnatural silence filled the room. The only sound came from the man behind the counter at the far end calling out numbers every now and then.

'We're not going to get out of here in a hurry,' whispered George. Alfreda nodded. It didn't worry her. She sat there and looked around the room, at the silent muffled characters, the jovial man busying himself behind the counter and at a strange stained glass window to her right, which depicted a young woman in a long white robe. Behind the young woman were green fields and woods and, in the distance, what looked like a factory. Underneath was an inscription in Latin that Alfreda didn't understand. Her attention was then caught by a man who came flustering into the room in very dramatic style. He sat down quickly in the row behind, wringing his hands and fidgeting nervously. Alfreda stared at him. He was wearing a dark, heavy suit and two thick scarves wrapped around his neck. He was far too anxious to notice Alfreda.

When she got bored with this she decided to rewind the tape of her memory and try and work out exactly where it was she had lost her voice. She'd certainly had it that morning. She remembered the conversation she'd had with Reg as she was getting ready for school. At the time he was sitting just outside her bedroom scratching himself behind the left ear . . .

Chapter 2

Reg was sitting outside the door to Alfreda's bedroom scratching himself behind the left ear and watching her getting ready for school. He had come upstairs to escape from George who had arrived in the kitchen, in dressing-gown and slippers, given Reg an over-enthusiastic pat on the head as he lay in his basket and begun singing a selection of songs from his favourite operettas while preparing the breakfast. This was all too much for a bleary-eyed Reg. He heaved himself out of his basket and trundled upstairs wondering all the time how it was possible for anybody to be quite so cheerful first thing in the morning.

He had hoped to find some peace and quiet on Alfreda's bed. Instead he found even more commotion, as Alfreda tried to stuff her schoolbooks into her bag and wrestled with the bedclothes to make them look neat. Simply watching all this feverish activity was enough to tire Reg out. He had to lie down. When Alfreda noticed him she said:

'Morning, Veg. Come to give me a hand?'

An irritated look came over the old dog's face, and Alfreda realised she'd probably have to apologise again. She had coined the name 'Reg the Veg' because he was getting so fat she thought he looked like a potato on legs. She knew he didn't find this funny. In fact, it was an affront to his dignity. And she usually ended up having to apologise or make amends.

'How can I give you a hand? I'm a dog, remember? Besides I have to conserve my strength.'

Alfreda was rather taken aback by this.

'Conserve your strength! What for?'

'I have a full and active day ahead of me.'

'Huh! A full and active stomach, that's all you've got!'

Reg was not going to let himself be provoked by this insult.

'You don't seem to realise,' he said, 'what great responsibilities lie on my shoulders. It's up to me to protect the lives and property of all those who live in this house.'

Alfreda let out a short laugh of disbelief. She had seen Reg in a good many different moods lately. There was Reg the Great Lover, for instance. For several days he had wandered around the house with a red rose between his teeth and Alfreda had even caught him in front of the mirror trying to teach himself how to wink. This phase came to an end when the petals fell off his rose and he never did learn how to wink properly. After that came Reg the Intrepid Explorer. From her bedroom window, Alfreda would often see him crashing around in the flower beds of the back garden searching for the Source of the Nile and being attacked from time to time by savage natives in the guise of Marjorie who would chase him with a broom and shout at him for trampling on her shrubs. But Reg the Security Guard! This was a new one!

Alfreda stood with her hands on her hips and said in a very sarcastic tone of voice:

'So you don't really spend all day snoring your head off. You're just pretending to be asleep to fool all those burglars who break in.'

Reg put his nose in the air and gave Alfreda a look of disdain.

'I admit that I do doze off from time to time, but that's only

...use I hate being idle. I go to sleep to give myself ...ething to do in those spare moments.'

Alfreda stood there speechless. She couldn't believe that Reg believed that she believed all this drivel he was talking. But, before she had the opportunity to reply, Reg was turning to leave, saying:

'Now, if you'll excuse me, I must continue my morning patrol. I still have the bathroom to check out.'

Reg lumbered off to see if there were any murderers or international terrorists in the airing cupboard, all the while thinking to himself that he ought to get a pair of dark glasses so he would look a lot more mean.

So Alfreda still had her voice when she left home that morning because she not only remembered talking with Reg, but also trying unsuccessfully to persuade her mother that she was still far too ill to go to school. She also remembered having it when she got on the school bus . . .

As she climbed aboard, she looked up and down the rows of seats to spot the familiar faces. She shouted to April and Sheila, then saw Parkway towards the back of the bus. He was waving to her.

'I saved you a place, Alf,' he said as she reached him.

Parkway shifted over to sit next to the window and Alfreda sat down beside him. He saved her a place every morning.

'Here,' said Alfreda, 'I've got some riddles for you.'

The bus journey to school in the morning usually took about twenty minutes. During that time, Alfreda asked Parkway no fewer than thirteen riddles, including the one about what's the difference between a fish and a lavatory seat, what d'you get if you cross a budgie with a flame-thrower, and why did the idiot take a ruler to bed with him? Parkway didn't get a single one right. Even when he had heard the riddle before and thought he knew the right answer, Alfreda would come up with a different answer which she said was definitely the correct one. In the end Parkway was beginning to wonder why he bothered.

As the bus drew up outside the school gates, Al
up and said to her friend:

'You're a bit of a pinhead when it comes to riddles,
you Parkway! Nobody'd guess you were a boffin!'

Parkway pulled a face at Alfreda and it suddenly occurred
him why he enjoyed doing maths.

'At least with maths there's only one answer. You get it
right or you get it wrong. With your riddles I never know how
many answers there are. And anyway, you keep changing
them all the time.'

'Anyone who likes maths wants his head examined,' said
Alfreda.

'One day I'll know the answer to all your riddles and there
won't be any point in asking me any more. You'll never be
able to catch me out again.'

Alfreda laughed.

'I'll just make up some new ones,' she said.

Alfreda and Parkway made their way across the playground
and joined a group of friends standing around chatting,
laughing and arguing, huddled together trying to stay warm,
their shoulders hunched, looking from behind like a circle of
penguins. Some were blowing on their hands through their
gloves, while others stood and watched their breath take on
the shape and form of long, white plumes of vapour as it came
in contact with the cold morning air.

There was no doubt that Alfreda still had her voice for
morning school. She was told off four times for talking too
much and twice for being disruptive. In the end she decided
she really ought to make some sort of comment on this state of
affairs. So she did:

'Some of the boys talk a lot more than me and they never get
told off.'

'That's because they usually have something interesting to
say,' replied her teacher.

Alfreda was not altogether convinced by this argument.

'Huh! That's not true. All they ever talk about is stupid,
old . . .'

'Just quiet down, Alfreda,' interrupted the teacher before
she could go any further. Not that that stopped her from going
further.

...ink motorbikes and things like that is ...hink it's dead boring.'
...die Jennings decided to join in.

...hat girls talk about,' he said with a sneer.

... to object to this too, but she thought
...dn't mind arguing with teachers, but
...argument with Eddie Jennings was about as
...ible as trying to dance with a charging rhinoceros.

'Alfreda, shut up and get on with your work. I won't tell you again,' said her teacher. So that's what she did, and had to be content with saying 'Go boil your head, Eddie!' in such a quiet voice that even April sitting next to her didn't hear.

When the lunch bell rang, Alfreda and Parkway went off to the dinner hall and joined in the pushing, prodding, elbowing, jostling queue. At the serving hatch, Alfreda took a tray.

'Now, Parkway, what are we going to have today?' she asked. 'Some curried mouse perhaps? Or bone stew?'

A dinner lady stood there looking at the two of them. She had a metal ladle in one hand, a metal lid in the other, and a weary expression on her face. In this pose she reminded Alfreda of a member of the school orchestra. The clanking and scratching noise she made with the two instruments in her hands made her sound like a member of the school orchestra too!

'The mouse looks very tasty,' said Parkway.

'Come on you two. Make up your mind. There's others waiting to be served,' said the dinner lady.

'Stew please,' said Alfreda.

The dinner lady landed a dollop of stew on Alfreda's plate.

'You don't have to eat it,' she said.

Alfreda and Parkway sat down at a nearby table.

'Eat up, Parkway,' said Alfreda in a tone of voice that sounded very much like her mother talking. 'If you don't finish your stew today, it will magically turn into a hamburger overnight and you'll have to eat it tomorrow.'

It occurred to Alfreda that she might have lost her voice in the playground after lunch. When afternoon school began her throat had felt rather sore from coughing a lot, which was due

16

to running around too much in the cold air. [When she came to]
think of it, it couldn't have been in the playgr[ound]
because she remembered talking to Mrs William[s, her]
teacher, about her poem . . .

Mrs Williams was giving back the poems she had take[n,]
occasionally reading through those she enjoyed. She came [to]
one and said:

'This one doesn't have a name on it, although I'm pretty
sure who wrote it.'

She began reading:

> I eat my dog with relish
> I like the taste a lot.
> A sausage dog is good when cold,
> He's even better hot.
>
> I put him into water,
> And boil him through and through.
> If he's not nice and tender,
> He's difficult to chew.
>
> He looks so pink and juicy
> As he lies in his bread roll.
> I cover him in ketchup
> And onions from a bowl.
>
> Now I've finished eating him
> I still don't feel full up.
> I wish I'd bought a bigger one,
> Not just a little pup.

'Is this one of your offerings, Alfreda?'

'Yeah,' she replied with a grin.

'I asked you to write a poem about an animal. I don't think
writing a poem about eating your dog is a very suitable
choice.'

'It's only a joke,' she sighed. 'It's not a real dog. It's a hot
dog.'

Alfreda found it extraordinary that it was necessary to
explain these things to adults all the time.

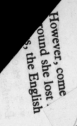

Abbot, I couldn't be sure if you were

as rather unfair. Eating Reg! The
ever eat Reg. He'd be far too tough!
debt of gratitude. After all, he had
this, the best poem she had ever
ay thought so. He was very keen on
his one he thought so good he wanted
could keep it . . .

Yes, that was it . . . it suddenly clicked . . . As she got off the bus home from school, Parkway had asked her for a copy of her poem and when she had tried to reply, nothing came out. Her mother must have been right. She probably did lose her voice on the bus. Not that knowing this made Alfreda feel any better.

Chapter 3

Father and daughter had been sitting in the Lost Voice Office for some time now, and Alfreda could sense that George's patience was beginning to drain away. The situation wasn't helped by the man sitting in the row behind them. He was wriggling and shifting about in his seat, looking up every now and then to see how many people were still ahead of him in the queue. This was getting on George's nerves and he turned round and gave him a dirty look. But it made no difference. The man seemed thoroughly disdainful and with each minute his anxiety seemed to grow.

'He's a bit full of himself!' George thought.

A few moments later, a strange noise grew out of the silence of the room—the rumbling of George's stomach. To take his mind off his hunger and the nervous shuffling in the row behind him, George tried thinking of other things. He began to wonder what life would be like if Alfreda's voice failed to turn up. Just think of it! The peace and quiet! No longer would he have to put up with the stream of nonsense that poured out of her mouth. It seemed to him that the older Alfreda got, the more empty-headed she was becoming. He didn't mind a little bit of nonsense now and again, but with Alfreda it was endless, relentless. It began the moment he got home in the evening. He'd be sitting quietly reading the newspaper in the kitchen after a hard day's work when Alfreda would appear . . . . . .

'Hi, Dad,' she said, sitting down at the table opposite him. All she could see of her father was eight fingers and the thinning hair on the top of his head. The rest was hidden behind the newspaper. George's voice floated out from behind the paper:

'Evening, Alfreda.'

Alfreda leant forward across the table and looked at the back and front pages of the newspaper that faced her. She began reading the headlines of stories, picking them out at random from here and there:

QUEEN OPENS PARLIAMENT
TOP EXECUTIVE RESIGNS
FIRE DESTROYS FISH AND CHIP SHOP.

'It says here,' she said to her father, 'the Queen's got fed up with her job and's going to run a fish and chip shop instead!'

George's voice floated out from behind the newspaper again.

'Don't be silly, Alfreda. I know you're just making that up. And I was always told it's rude to read other people's newspapers while they're reading them.'

'Just a joke,' said Alfreda with a slight shrug of the shoulders.

'Elbows off the table, dear,' said Marjorie, putting a bowl of spaghetti down. 'And don't annoy your father. He's had a long day at the office.'

Alfreda had never understood what it was about her elbows that meant she couldn't keep them on the table. They weren't unhygienic in any way. Nor were they so heavy or pointed that they might make dents in the table. So why were adults so concerned about elbows? Her grandfather had told her that the only thing she was allowed to put in her ear was her elbow. Everything else was forbidden. She hadn't understood *that* either.

When the spaghetti had been served up, Alfreda struggled valiantly to get some off her plate and into her mouth. Either she picked up too little and it slipped off her fork, or she picked up far too much. Sucking one strand at a time was more successful, except that the final section would often flick her across the nose before disappearing, spattering her face with flecks of tomato sauce. George Abbot looked across at his daughter who was sitting there with little red dots all over her face. He sighed.

'You'd have thought at your age you'd have learnt how to eat properly!'

'Can't help it. Stupid stuff,' said Alfreda wiping her face. 'What's the point of eating food that attacks you?'

Marjorie decided to change the subject. When George began making comments about Alfreda's eating habits it usually ended in a row.

'What did you do at school today?' she asked.

'The usual. Moths. Borology. Histerics. Had a game of Notball. In Histerics we learned all about this woman who rode around the countryside with knives sticking out of her chariot cutting Romans in half.'

'I don't suppose you remember what her name was?' said George, laying down his fork.

Alfreda folded her arms, knitted her brow and thought for a moment.

'Er .... no,' she replied.

'Queen Boadicea, or to be more precise, Boudicca.'

Alfreda burst out laughing. Boudicca! She was glad she wasn't called Boudicca. Alfreda was bad enough. But Boudicca . . .! Boudicca Abbot! It just didn't bear thinking about. George, on the other hand, failed to see what was so funny about this. He shook his head.

'It's about time you started paying more attention to your school work. What's the point of learning something if you simply forget it ten minutes later. You really must start taking things a little more seriously.'

'Sorry, Dad. Didn't mean to laugh.'

There was a lull in the conversation during which time Alfreda decided to attack this spaghetti in a different way. It certainly wasn't going to get the better of her. She fetched herself a knife from the drawer and, having hacked the spaghetti into manageable lengths, she ate it with a spoon. The meal continued in silence, which was finally broken by Alfreda saying:

'Anyway, me and Parkway thought we'd give it a go on Saturday morning in the High Street.'

'Give what a go?' asked Marjorie, rather alarmed.

'Doing what whats'ername did. We're going to fix knives to our bikes and ride up and down the shopping precinct. We're going to call ourselves "The Shopper Choppers". I thought up that name,' said Alfreda proudly.

'I don't think that's a very nice idea,' said Marjorie, looking somewhat taken aback. And she added:

'I always thought that Parkway was such a quiet, sensible boy. I can't imagine him doing such a thing!'

'You haven't been watching one of those video nasties, have you?' George asked.

Alfreda raised her eyebrows and sighed:

'It's only a joke. Parkway can't even ride a bike.'

'Mmmmmm,' said George suspiciously. 'Well, whether it's a joke or not, I don't like you telling fibs.'

After supper, Alfreda managed to avoid doing the washing-up by mumbling some excuse about not having finished her homework. When George and Marjorie went into the sitting room some twenty minutes later, they found Alfreda lying on the floor in front of the television with Reg sitting beside her. Both were staring unblinkingly at the glowing screen.

'I thought you had homework to do,' said George.

'Done it,' said Alfreda without looking away from the television.

Although George didn't like Alfreda watching too much television, at least it kept her quiet for a while.

Alfreda, however, was getting bored. She'd seen this programme before and didn't like it much the first time. Reg, on the other hand, seemed engrossed, so she left him there and went up to her bedroom to fetch a book. She reappeared a few moments later and sat cross-legged on the carpet to read.

On the inside front cover of Alfreda's book was written the following inscription:

> To Alfreda,
> who I know will enjoy this book because its all about people without an ounce of sense in their heads
>
> Love Uncle Harry

The book was a present from George's younger brother. He had left school at fourteen and spent many years travelling the world. For some of that time he had been a seaman in the Merchant Navy and for the rest he had found jobs when and where he could. Recently he had returned to the town of his birth and, with the money he had saved over the years, had bought himself a small general store not far from where George, Marjorie and Alfreda lived.

Alfreda flicked through the pages of the book until she found the story she was looking for. She turned the sound down on the television which annoyed Reg because it was his favourite quiz show, and she began reading:

There was once a poor man who had spent almost all his life living alone in the forest. One day he resolved to leave the forest and set out for the City in the hope that he might make his fortune there. After many days' travel, he came within sight of the City. But the roads which led into it were crowded with people. He looked at this great crowd and at once became anxious. He said to himself: I might easily lose myself among all these people. And if I do, how am I going to find myself again? I must have something about me which the others do not. So saying, he found a pumpkin at the side of the road. He tied the pumpkin to his left leg as a way of recognising himself and made his way into the City. Once inside, he marvelled at everything he saw and in the course of his wanderings through the streets, he was befriended by a mischievous young man. This rogue took it upon himself to be the poor man's guide and, come nightfall, he offered him a bed for the night in his own house.

During the night, while the poor man slept, the young man removed the pumpkin from his visitor's leg, attached it to his own, and returned to bed. In the morning the poor man woke up and saw the pumpkin attached to his companion's leg.

'Hey, wake up you!' he said, 'if you are you! I am very confused. For, if you are you with the pumpkin attached, then you must be me! In which case, who am I?'

The poor man stood there in a state of . . . .

'Is that the book Uncle Harry gave you?' asked Marjorie, interrupting Alfreda's reading.

'Yeah. It's dead good.'

'What's it about?'

'Oh, just a lot of stupid blokes doing stupid things.'

'It sounds exactly the sort of book that Harry would enjoy,' said George sarcastically.

Alfreda was about to go back to her reading when her father asked:

'I hope you don't bother Harry or get in his way when you go round to see him.'

'Don't think so. I help him out in his shop and he tells me stories about his travels and things like that.'

'Most of those should be taken with a large pinch of salt,' said George.

'And he teaches me about all sorts of things,' said Alfreda.

'Oh yes! What sort of things?' There was a hint of suspicion in George's voice.

'Well,' said Alfreda, 'the last time I went round there he was telling me all about the Law and that.'

George sat up in his chair with a smile on his face.

'So you and Uncle Harry spend your time discussing legal matters, do you?'

'Yeah.'

'And what does Harry know about the Law?'

'Well, for example,' Alfreda explained, 'he says that if you post a piece of coal through somebody's letter box, that's blackmail!' George looked at his daughter and shook his head:

'You know, for one moment, I thought you were going to say something interesting.'

'And,' Alfreda continued, 'if you kill yourself by a sewer, it's sewerside.'

George sank back into his chair and sighed:

'It was silly of me to expect anything different, I suppose.'

'And,' Alfreda continued, 'if you pick your nose on Sunday . . . .'

'All right Alfreda. That's more than enough, thank you.'

George shook open his newspaper and sat looking cross. This was absolutely typical of Alfreda's behaviour, and who could blame him for feeling exasperated by it. At the same time Reg turned to Alfreda and gave her a sly grin, which she returned. The room was filled with the sound of laughter and applause from Reg's favourite quiz show.

'And that dog watches far too much television,' said George sharply. 'He'll ruin his eyesight, if he hasn't done so already.'

Reg was on the verge of poking his tongue out at George, but he thought better of it and decided to ignore him instead. Marjorie got to her feet and announced that she was going to make some coffee, and Alfreda went back to her book. No sooner had she found the page where she had left off than her attention was suddenly caught by a rather unpleasant smell that was drifting around her. It was difficult at first to make out exactly where it had come from. Then she looked at Reg, who was behaving as if nothing had happened. This made Alfreda suspicious. She shuffled across the carpet and sat next to him, staring at him intensely. Reg ignored this intrusion and went on watching the television. Then Alfreda whispered in his ear:

'Reg! Have you been talking with your bottom? You just farted, didn't you?'

There was no reaction at all from Reg, who pretended he hadn't heard a word. George, on the other hand, who wasn't meant to have heard, did and exploded:

'Alfreda! I will not have you using that sort of language in this house! Do you understand?'

Alfreda had never been very good at whispering. She had difficulty controlling the volume of her voice. Now it had got her into trouble again. And, as whenever she got into trouble, the first thing she tried to do was to blame it on somebody else.

'It wasn't me. It was Reg's fault. He did it. Tell him off!'

'I'm not going to argue with you,' replied her father. 'I've made myself clear. Sometimes you just go too far.'

Alfreda paused for a moment, then said:

'Sorry, Dad.'

When Marjorie returned, pushing open the door with the tray, she could sense the uneasy atmosphere in the room. George was looking sullen and irritated, and Alfreda was pouting. As she put the tray down on the table she thought to herself: 'I can't leave them alone for two minutes without them bickering with one another.'

Some time later, after Alfreda had gone to bed and George was enjoying the quiet that came with her absence, he stretched out in his chair and put his hands behind his head.

'What is the matter with that girl?' he asked his wife.

'What do you mean?' she replied, flicking over a page of the magazine she was looking at.

'When's she going to start growing up, that's what I want to know? When's she going to get over all this nonsense she talks? She doesn't pay any attention to her schoolwork and her language is getting worse every day. It's about time she started behaving a little more sensibly.'

'I think you're being a bit hard on her, George. She's still only young.'

'I was never that frivolous when I was her age! She's going to have to learn sooner or later that life is a serious business.'

'Yes, George.'

'You know what I think?' asked George.

'Yes, George.'

'It's partly Harry's influence. That's what I think. He's as bad as she is, and he should know better.'

'Yes, George,' said Marjorie, slowly turning another page. 'Well, I think you're just going to have to be a bit more patient. After all, nothing is going to change overnight.'

Chapter 4

The man behind the counter at the Lost Voice Office called
out another number. It broke the silence of the room and
interrupted George's thoughts. He calculated that there were
still seventeen more people in front of them. It would be a
while yet before Alfreda's turn came round. She, meanwhile,
was staring at the bloke in the row behind again. He had taken
off his scarves and was energetically biting his nails. She
grinned at him and he scowled back. She turned round when
her father tapped her on the shoulder and whispered:

'I hope your voice is here after all this waiting.'

Alfreda shrugged. She was feeling a little guilty that her
father had had to sit here all this time. On the other hand, she
felt annoyed that he was making such a fuss about it.

George settled down and resigned himself to the long wait.
His thoughts returned to what Marjorie had said. He decided
she was probably right. Alfreda's behaviour wasn't going to
change overnight. However he was still convinced that Harry
was a bad influence.

It must be said that George and Harry didn't get on very well together. It had come as a bit of a shock to George when his younger brother had reappeared suddenly after so many years without hearing from him, not even knowing whether he was dead or alive. And it was even more of a shock when Harry announced that he was going to be living not very far away. Although the two brothers had been close when they were young, during the many years of absence they had grown apart, gone their separate ways, and had now become strangers to one another. George found it difficult to understand Harry's carefree attitude, especially when it came to business. As he said to Marjorie one day:

'He runs that shop in a most unbusiness-like manner. He lets people buy on credit. He even gives things away. He'll end up bankrupt, you mark my words, unless he starts taking the enterprise a bit more seriously.'

Strangely enough, at that very moment, as Alfreda sat next to her father in the Lost Voice Office, she too was thinking about Uncle Harry. But it wasn't the way he ran his shop that concerned her. No, the thing that interested Alfreda was his tattoos. These had impressed her greatly the first time they met . . .

'I got this one in Shanghai, from a little Chinese bloke who never stopped smiling.'

Harry rolled up his shirtsleeve and showed Alfreda his upper arm. On it was printed a bright green and purple dragon. Harry could make it twist and writhe on his arm by flexing his muscles. This gave Alfreda the creeps:

'Ugggghhhhhh! It's horrible,' she shrieked, convinced the creature really had come to life. It was a trick Alfreda never got tired of.

Nor did she tire of Harry's stories. He seemed to have an endless stock of them; the tales of a seafaring man. He would tell her of the strange and exotic lands he had been to, the dangers he had encountered, the curious characters he had met and the extraordinary sights he had witnessed. The number of stories was matched only by the supply of jokes and riddles that Harry kept. These appealed to Alfreda no end, as she could try them out on friends at school.

'The thing about jokes,' said Harry to Alfreda one day as he tossed her an apple from a tray outside his shop, 'is that they've got to be fresh. Otherwise, they're just not funny. Nobody's interested in stale old jokes.'

Alfreda examined the rather dried-up, withered apple she had caught and said:

'And I reckon this apple is even older than some of your jokes!'

So Alfreda looked forward eagerly to Saturday mornings, which was when she and Parkway would go round to Harry's to help him out in the shop. They would meet up at the corner of the street and make their way together to the general store. It was not very far away as the crow flies, but it always took them a curiously long time to walk the distance involved. This was because they had to find their way through a maze of narrow backstreets, all of which looked similar to one another. Parkway remembered one occasion when he almost got completely lost among these streets, even though he knew all the time that he was close to home. By now, of course, the two friends had no difficulty in finding Harry's shop, although for anybody who did not know its whereabouts, tucked away amid a row of terraced houses, it was easy to miss.

The shop looked no size at all from the outside, but inside not an inch of space was wasted. The shelving went from floor to ceiling and, despite its size, the shop sold just about everything anyone could possibly wish for, from toothpicks to broomhandles, from hair oil to loo paper, from Chinese rice to Indian tea, from birthday candles to rat poison. In fact it was a bit of a mystery how so much got packed into such a small space.

The arrival of Alfreda and Parkway was announced by the tinkling of a small bell above their heads as they stepped through the door. At that moment Harry was up a step-ladder, stacking the top shelf with bags of flour. He came down the ladder to greet his two assistants.

'You arrived just in time,' he said. 'I need a couple of extra pairs of hands. The first thing we'll do is finish off packing this shelf.'

Alfreda, Parkway and Harry formed a chain. Alfreda took

the bags out of a large cardboard box and handed them one at a time to Parkway who was on the second rung of the ladder. He in turn handed them up to Harry at the top, who stacked them into the space provided. When this task was finished the three of them stood admiring their handiwork, five rows of bags of flour packed like soft, fat bricks. Looking up and down the shelves, Harry remarked:

'These shelves remind me of the decks of an ocean-going liner. And it's always on the bottom deck here that all the work gets done.'

Alfreda liked the idea of a shop that looked like a ship, and it amused her that Harry had spent most of his life either on a ship or in a shop.

Next, the two assistants had to go and fetch three sacks of potatoes from the storeroom adjoining the shop and put them out on the pavement next to the fruit and vegetables that were on display there. Meanwhile, Harry went off into the backroom to mend a fuse. As he was unscrewing the plug, he could hear the sound of groaning, puffing and panting coming from his two employees as they struggled to drag, heave and shove the heavy sacks through the shop and out of the door. These noises of strain and exertion were interrupted every now and again by a burst of laughter, or by Parkway shouting that the sack was on his foot, or by Alfreda complaining that she was doing all the work.

When Harry had screwed the plug back together again, he went to find out how the other two had got on. They were sitting on the front step getting their breath back. Outside on the pavement the sacks of brown cloth stood propped up, leaning against each other like three snoozing tramps.

'Good work, mates,' said Harry with a smile.

'Hope we don't have to do that again,' said Alfreda. 'Too much like hard work! I'd rather get the sack than get the sacks.'

Alfreda burst into uncontrollable laughter at this joke, which she was sure was the best joke anybody had cracked in at least the last two hundred years. Harry and Parkway, however, did not share this opinion. They tutted and pulled a face.

'Don't laugh at your own jokes, Alfreda,' said Parkway.

'If *she* doesn't nobody else will,' said Harry.

Then Harry suggested they take a break, so that they could recover both from the exertions of the morning and from Alfreda's dreadful joke. The three of them went through to the backroom just off the shop behind the counter.

Harry made some tea and brought in some biscuits, but the tinkling of the bell meant he had to go and serve the customer who had just come in. Alfreda sat stroking Rover, Harry's cat, and Parkway moved around the room looking at the numerous maps which all but covered the walls. He tried pronouncing some of the strange-sounding place names he came across and followed the black dotted lines of the sea-lanes with his finger.

'Did you know it takes thirty-two hours to get from Athens to Istanbul by ship?' he asked.

' 'Course I did,' replied Alfreda in a bored tone of voice as if it was the sort of thing that everybody knew.

'Liar,' said Parkway.

'Don't believe me then,' Alfreda said with a shrug of her shoulders.

Harry returned to the backroom and poured the tea. As he handed a mug to Alfreda he said:

'You know, those sacks of potatoes remind me of a time, when was it? I went to visit an old friend of mine, Baron von Munchhausen.'

'Baron von who?' said Alfreda in a tone of disbelief.

'Baron Karl von Munchhausen.'

'You don't know any Barons,' she said dismissively.

Harry looked hurt that his niece should doubt his word.

'O.K.,' he said. 'Ask me anything you like about him. Come on. What do you want to know?'

'Can you show me where the Baron lived?' asked Parkway who was still gazing at a map of the world.

'Certainly,' said Harry. And he went over to the map and pointed to a large empty space in the middle of Germany.

'But there's nothing there,' protested Parkway.

'It's only a very small town,' said Harry. 'They wouldn't bother to mark it on a map of this scale. The Baron's house was perched on a rock high above the town overlooking the surrounding countryside. And all you could see for miles around was thick forest, nothing but pine trees as far as the horizon.'

Harry paused for a moment looking at nothing in particular, or maybe in his mind he was looking out over that forest again. After a while he continued:

'The Baron was an old man when *I* knew him. He must be even older by now.'

'What did he look like?' asked Alfreda. 'And where did you meet him?'

'I first came across him in a bookshop in Cairo. He was a short, square man, but he stood very upright. He had a very straight, stiff back. I remember he was wearing a suit of dark blue cloth. In fact he looked very dull and ordinary at first glance, but once I got talking to him he was transformed. He'd led a remarkable life, full of travel and adventure. He could talk for hours about where he'd been and what he'd done.'

Alfreda was looking rather puzzled at this point and she interrupted:

'Harry, what's all this got to do with sacks of potatoes?'

'Oh yes, the sacks. I'd almost forgotten about them. Yes. That time I went to visit him. We were sitting by his fire talking over old times and I asked him about the town that you could see down below from his house. It turned out to be a very curious place, or rather a place full of very odd people. The Baron told me about the time the inhabitants decided to build a large hall where the Town Council could meet. They had no problem building the walls and raising the roof timbers, which were then covered in slates. When the last slate was fixed in place, the whole town gathered inside the Council Hall. But it wasn't long before somebody realised that something was wrong. Inside the building it was pitch dark. One man said that he couldn't see his hand in front of his face and a woman asked how the Town Council was expected to make enlightened decisions when the Council Hall was as black as night. So they all sat down and had a think about it and finally one of them came up with the solution. They would take the roof off! This is not as silly as it sounds. In fact it worked very well—during the summer. When the snows and wind and rain of winter came they realised they would have to think of something else. So they put the roof back on and sat and thought some more. Then one of them, who was noted for being more intelligent than most, announced that he had found the perfect solution. He told everybody to assemble outside the Hall each carrying a sack. He then explained what they had to do. Each person had to fill their sack with light from outside, take it into the Hall and empty it in there. Then they had to fill their sack with darkness from the Hall, bring it outside and throw it away. Thus all the darkness would be removed from the Hall and eventually it would become filled with light.'

Harry leaned back in his chair and scratched his beard. He looked at Alfreda and Parkway who looked at Harry who was looking at Alfreda and Parkway.

'Well?' said Alfreda. 'What happened then?'

Harry leaned forward in his chair towards Alfreda and said:

'That's exactly what I asked the Baron.'

Alfreda was getting impatient.

'Well! What did he say?'

'He pulled a face and said he hadn't been down to the town for years so he wasn't sure what the outcome was. But, as far as he knew, the plan with the sacks hadn't made a blind bit of difference. The Council Hall was still as dark as ever.'

'That's the daftest story I've ever heard,' said Alfreda enthusiastically. 'Did he tell you any more, the Baron?'

'He could talk the hind legs off a donkey. In fact the local townspeople used to lock up their donkeys whenever they saw him coming!'

Harry searched through his memory for all the stories the Baron had ever told him, and the telling of one brought to mind the memory of another, such that he could have gone on for over three years if another customer had not come into the shop. Harry went off to serve him and when he returned Alfreda deluged him with questions about this acquaintance of his. Important questions like what colour were his socks, did he have any pets, could he eat spaghetti with just a fork?

'There wasn't much he couldn't do,' said Harry. 'He could fly a plane and, by all accounts, he was an Olympic toboggan champion. He went mountain-climbing in the Alps and tiger-hunting in India. Apparently he was a crack shot.'

'Sounds more like a crackpot to me,' said Alfreda.

Harry ignored this interruption and continued:

'It's said he could speak fifty-six languages as well, some of them only known to himself. He was the only person alive who knew how to speak them.'

Alfreda liked this idea.

'So he could be rude to anybody he liked and they'd never know!' she said.

'Can you speak any other languages, Mr Abbot?' asked Parkway.

'Oh, I've picked up a few words here and there. You're bound to if you travel a lot. But I never stayed put in one place long enough to learn any languages properly. I'll tell you about the strangest language I ever came across though. I was working as a stoker on a cargo ship that was carrying things between some islands in the South Pacific—oil drums, pineapples, that sort of thing.'

Parkway insisted on being shown where these islands were on the map he was gazing at. Harry, with Alfreda and Parkway on either side of him, scanned the map for a moment. Then with his finger he joined up the dots of a pattern of islands that sat in the middle of a vast expanse of blue. At the fifth dot his finger stopped and he tapped the map.

'Here,' he said, 'this was the island. We'd docked there for a couple of days to off-load some cargo and take on fresh supplies. I was doing a bit of sightseeing, wandering around the little harbour, when I overheard two of the islanders talking to each other as they sat under a tree. I didn't understand anything of what they were saying, but what was curious was that every now and then they made this sort of beeping noise at each other. It was like they were saying: "Hello beep. What a nice beep beep day beep." '

Alfreda and Parkway fell about at Harry's impression of what this strange language sounded like.

'But why did they do that?' asked Alfreda.

'I had no idea. And I reckoned there was only one person who might know. He was the first mate. He'd lived among those islands for a long time, so he knew them as well as anyone. I told him what I'd heard and asked him what it was all about. He said that nobody really knew where the beep language had come from, and he'd only ever come across one explanation. Apparently, during the last war, the island had been occupied by Japanese soldiers and when they retreated one of them must have forgotten or abandoned a morse code machine in the jungle. Some islanders must have found the machine and taken it back to their village where it probably started transmitting, talking to them in a series of beeps. They must have thought it was one of their gods talking to them because they built a temple for the machine in the middle of the village. The mate said if I went to the village I could still see the little god in his temple. Anyway, the Chief and the priests used to go into the temple and talk to the machine in beeps, hoping it would answer back. And soon the other villagers were making up songs about it. So beeping became part of their everyday speech, although, according to the first mate, the Chief and the priests tried to stop ordinary villagers from beeping. They thought that only important people like themselves should be allowed to beep.'

'Blimey!' said Alfreda, 'you have met some odd characters!'

'I suppose so,' replied Harry, 'only they don't really seem so at the time. It's just what you're used to. To some people it might seem strange that we open up packets full of dry, black leaves which have come from a far-off country where they are specially grown and picked and packaged and transported thousands of miles just so we can pour boiling water over them and drink them.'

'Yeah, does sound a bit daft,' Alfreda admitted.

At that moment another customer came into the shop.

'Right,' said Harry. 'Enough chat for one morning. Back to work.'

While Harry served the man who had come into the shop Alfreda and Parkway set about their appointed tasks. He had to tidy up and sweep out the storeroom. She had to put price labels on any items that didn't have any. As usual, Alfreda got carried away. At the end of three quarters of an hour there were prices all over the shop. Rover was trying to shake one off her paws, Parkway had several on the back of his anorak and Alfreda had even managed to attach one to Harry's beard without his noticing. He only found out when an old woman who had come into the shop to buy some cough sweets offered to buy his beard as well. She said she could stick it on her husband's chest and perhaps he'd stop getting these colds every winter. Harry turned to Alfreda and said:

'I can see I'm going to have to enforce stricter discipline among this crew.'

Alfreda grinned and saluted.

At one o'clock Harry shut up the shop and his two assistants prepared to go home for lunch. But first there was the important matter of wages to settle. Alfreda spent many minutes surveying the sweets counter before deciding on what to take. She changed her mind half a dozen times before she finally said:

'No, I'll definitely have a packet of gubblebum.'

'Don't let your mother see it,' said Harry, 'or you'll get me into trouble. What about you, Parkway, old shipmate?'

'Crisps?' replied Parkway hesitantly. He was always uneasy about the idea that he could have whatever he wanted from the sweets counter. He often chose something cheap which he didn't really want rather than something expensive which he definitely did.

'Yeah, but what sort of flavour, Parkway?' asked Alfreda sarcastically. 'There are all sorts of different flavours, re-member?'

Alfreda bent down to inspect the boxes of crisps on the bottom shelf.

'There's pig flavour, and smoky buffalo flavour, my favourites! and old sock flavour . . . . Come on, Parkway. Make up your mind.'

'Got any plain ones?' asked Parkway.

'God, you're so boring Parkway!' said Alfreda and she chucked a packet of plain crisps across the shop to him.

Harry stood at the door of the shop and watched the two friends wander off down the street and disappear round the corner. All the while, Alfreda was telling Parkway how much she enjoyed working in the shop and what a good bloke Harry was and his stories were really interesting and Parkway said what he liked best were the maps and the foreign countries and Alfreda said yeah and the funny customs.

'Travelling the world!' said Parkway. There was an excitement in simply pronouncing the phrase. And as they made their way back along the usual route which would take them home, Alfreda said:

'It's got to be better than being stuck in this boring dump of a town!'

At the last corner the two friends parted company and went their separate ways.

George Abbot had spent all Saturday morning at the local Garden Centre buying shrubs and bedding plants to replace the ones Reg had destroyed in his search for the Source of the Nile. He arrived back at the house and almost fell in the front door under the weight of greenery he was carrying. As he stood in the hallway for a moment he said to his daughter who passed him on her way up to her room:

'Hello Alfreda.'

To which she replied:

'Beep beep.'

George went out into the back garden to find his wife. She was digging, lifting heavy sodden lumps of earth and then shaking the fork to try and unstick them.

'Marjorie,' said George, 'I just said hello to my daughter and she beeped at me. Do you have any idea why?'

Marjorie stood up and flicked a wayward piece of hair out of her face with a rubber-gloved hand.

'Apparently it's a new language Harry has taught her.'

'I might have known it!' said George. 'I might have known he'd be behind it!'

'Oh don't be so dramatic. She's only having a bit of fun.'

'A bit of fun! If you ask me she spends too much time having a bit of fun. I didn't go around beeping at people when I was her age. I certainly never beeped at my father. It's about time that girl started behaving more like a human being and less like an idiot!'

From her bedroom window, Alfreda could hear this conversation taking place. She shrugged her shoulders and, turning to Reg, she asked:

'Beebeebeep?'

To which Reg simply nodded and replied:

'Beeeebeep.'

Because, being a highly intelligent dog, he had no difficulty in picking up a new language very quickly.

Chapter 5

'At long last!' said George, rather more loudly than he had meant to. The man in front of them in the queue had got his voice back and was making for the door of the Lost Voice Office. George and Alfreda went up to the counter. The man behind the counter finished filling out a form and then turned towards father and daughter.

'Sorry about the delay, sir. Our busiest time of the year, this. Rushed off our feet we are! Now, which one of you has to be sorted out? The little girl?'

Alfreda scowled at him. She didn't like being called a little girl.

'My daughter,' said George.

'Name?'

'Alfreda Abbot.'

The man began filling in a fresh form. He wanted to know where Alfreda was born, when she was born, where she'd lived, where she lived now, where she went to school, where she'd been to school, whether she'd ever lived abroad, when and where she'd lost her voice, no end of details.

'Do you have the birth certificate, sir?'

George handed over the birth certificate, which the man glanced at before he strolled off into the rows of shelves behind him. He would disappear down one row of shelves only to reappear in another, all the time looking up and down, along and back, bobbing and ducking like a slow-motion boxer. He disappeared from view again, then returned to the counter, holding his official documents in one hand and a small, sealed plastic bag in the other. The bag had a very long number written on it.

'Here we are!'

The man tore open the plastic bag and removed what looked like a grey cornflake. He put the 'cornflake' onto a small metal plate below the counter and screwed a lid down tightly on top of it. He was just about to pull on a lever when George interrupted him:

'Excuse me a moment. I don't mean to be awkward, but . . how do we know that's my daughter's voice? All these voices look the same to me. How can you tell the difference between them?'

The man threw back his shoulders slightly and looked at George. He was obviously put out that anybody should question his ability to do his job.

'Years of training, sir,' he replied, indignantly. 'Could you recognise your own fingerprint? No, of course not. All fingerprints look the same to you, don't they! It takes an expert, a trained eye.' (Here the man pointed to his right eye.) 'Only a trained eye can spot the differences.'

George felt abashed and not a little embarrassed that he had doubted the man's expertise, although he hoped at the same time that his left eye was as highly trained as his right eye obviously was. The man shot George another withering glance to make him squirm a bit more, then he pulled on the lever. There was a low hissing sound to be heard from the machine, something like steam escaping.

'This is just to sterilise the voice. It's probably been lying around somewhere getting grubby. We don't want you using any dirty words, young lady, do we!'

George thought this was a very unsuitable thing to say in front of his daughter.

The Lost Voice Man lifted the lever, unscrewed the lid and handed the voice to its owner. It had been transformed into a brilliant white colour and it felt as light as a snowflake.

'Put that on your tongue and let it dissolve. It should be ready to use in about half an hour.'

Alfreda could feel the snowflake begin to dissolve the moment it touched her tongue.

As George left the Lost Voice Office with his daughter, he cast a final glance at the man who had been sitting behind them. By now he was almost shaking with impatience and looking constantly at his watch. To tell the truth, George began to feel rather sorry for him, he was in such a state!

'That man doesn't look very well,' he thought to himself. The man's name, although neither George nor Alfreda knew this, was Norbert S. Quire, Esq.

Chapter 6

BRRRBRRR . . . . .brrrbrrr . . . . .BRRRBRRR . . . . . .
. . .brrrbrrr . . . . .BRRRBRRR . . . . .

Mr Quire rose out of his armchair and went to answer the phone. He had to remove both the scarves from around his mouth before he tried to say: Good afternoon, Norbert S. Quire speaking. He tried, but he couldn't. Nothing came out. He tried again and this time managed a thin wheeze. The third time, not even the thin wheeze. Meanwhile the voice on the other end was sounding confused.

'Hello .... Hello .... Norbert? Are you there?'
'????'
'Norbert! .... This is Deirdre!'
'!!!!'
'I phoned earlier, but there was no reply.'
'!!??!'
'Norbert, I know you're there. I can hear you breathing.'
'???!!'

'You can be extremely childish at times . . . Don't bother phoning back because I don't want to talk to you.'

Click   Whhhhhhhhhhhhhhhrrrrrrrrrrrrrrrrrrrrrrrrrrrrrrrrr. The phone went dead.

Mr Quire stood there listening to the dead phone. It took a little while to sink in that he had lost his voice. It took a little longer to realise that he must have lost it on his walk.

Norbert Quire began to panic. His voice must be out *there* somewhere, lying in the fog. There was no chance of finding it, not in these conditions. There was no point in even looking for it. It could be anywhere. His only hope was that someone had found it and handed it in. But what if they didn't? What if it was never found? What if it was lost for good? All these thoughts flashed through Mr Quire's mind and made him go weak at the knees. He had never lost his voice before. He wasn't sure if he could cope. It had broken once. That had been bad enough. People kept laughing at him because his voice went up and down like a roller-coaster every time he spoke. Luckily it had mended after a while, but it was never the same again. Now he faced the prospect of having no voice at all! Mr Quire broke out in a cold sweat at this thought. No more performances, his career in ruins, nothing would remain of the glory his voice once had been. And what about the audition!!!!???? How was he going to audition without a voice? What chance did he stand of getting this part if he couldn't say a word? All this was more than Norbert Quire could bear. He fainted . . .

Since before he could remember, Mr Norbert Quire had felt unwell. Indeed from the very moment of his birth he'd been ill. The midwife who delivered him had picked him up by the ankles and slapped him on the bottom expecting to hear him bawl, to let out the first howl of life. Instead, all that issued from the tiny Norbert was a cough and a sneeze. A cold had been his constant companion from that moment on.

So there was nothing unusual about how he had been feeling earlier that morning when he woke up in his lofty wooden bed.

It was only after much deliberation and something of a struggle that Mr Quire had dragged himself out of bed and across his bedroom to the low chair where a dressing gown lay. He pulled it on over his shoulders. Then he drew back the long velvet curtains that covered the windows. He peered out of the window through half-closed eyes. All he could see was fog. He rubbed his eyes, then he rubbed the window pane. Still fog. A thick fog enveloped everything. The only thing he could make out was the glow from a street lamp which, like Mr Quire, was straining to pierce the gloom.

'Harrumph!' he said, with feeling.

Mr Quire went into his bathroom and inspected his face in the mirror. He stuck out his pale tongue and looked away. The last thing he wanted to face at that hour of the morning was his face. He opened a white medical cabinet and was almost buried under an avalanche of vitamin bottles.

'Damn and Blast!' he said, crawling around on his hands and knees picking up the bottles and popping the odd vitamin tablet into his mouth. He did this every morning. It made not the slightest difference to his health.

In the kitchen, Mr Quire made himself a pot of camomile tea and a look of disgust crossed his face as he poured it into a cup.

'Filthy stuff!' he muttered to himself. He had read somewhere that camomile tea did you good. In fact, as with the vitamins, it made him feel no better. He was just afraid that if he stopped drinking it he'd feel worse.

Mr Quire returned to his bedroom with his pot of tea and decided to go through his morning exercises. Today of all days he had to do his exercises!

1 Deep-breathing exercises. (These made Mr Quire dizzy.)
2 Gargling with mouthwash. (This made him choke.)
3 Spray with throat spray. (This made him cough.)
4 Vocal Exercises. (Mr Quire sang some musical scales, then made all sorts of strange sounds, from grunting to squeaking.)
5 Forty-six knee bends. (These made his knees swell up.)

Mr Quire hobbled over to the low chair and collapsed into it to recover.

These rather curious exercises, which he went through every morning, were designed to keep himself, and more importantly his voice, in peak condition. For Mr Norbert

Quire was an actor by profession and he took great care of his voice for that reason. He liked to think of his voice as 'A rich, ripe, red plum.' Although on that particular morning, after he'd done his exercises, it seemed more like 'A stale, old, dried-out biscuit.'

This worried Mr Quire a little, because that evening he was due to attend a very important audition—perhaps the most important audition of his career so far. A play called *The Secret of the Cave* was going to be staged at the theatre in the town and he desperately wanted the starring role, that of Sir John Tressillie—prosperous Gentleman, Soldier and Hero. This was a truly serious part, worthy of Mr Norbert Quire's great talents as a tragic actor. As he sat in his chair, recovering from his exertions, an image of himself began to form in Mr Quire's mind. There he was, standing on the stage, bowing deeply, and before him a packed audience, on its feet, roaring applause and wiping the tears from its eyes.

When Mr Quire had got dressed he went to the front door of his flat to see what the post had brought. On the mat lay a postcard from his Aunt Cecily inviting him to visit her, and a letter. He hurriedly opened the letter and read the contents.

Squibb's Theatrical Agency

27th November

Dear Mr Quire,

I am pleased to inform you that we can offer you the part of a frozen pea in a television commercial. You will be playing the role of a big, tough, old pea which gets rejected in favour of a small, sweet, young one. You will be paid the standard rate. Could you please attend the television studios on 14th December in plenty of time to be fitted with your pea costume.

Yours sincerely

Arnold Squibb

Mr Quire was outraged.

'**How dare he!**' he roared. '**To suggest that I, Norbert Quire, should play the part of a vegetable! The insolence of it!**'

Mr Quire tore the letter into shreds and scattered them on the floor.

'I suppose this is somebody's idea of a joke,' he muttered to himself. 'Huh! The day will come, never fear, the day will come when my name will be Honoured!'

In his hallway Mr Quire went slowly down on one knee, bowed his head, and in solemn voice said:

'For your services to the Theatre, arrrrise, Sir Norbert!'

A sudden bang on the front door and Sir Norbert arose at high speed, as if he'd knelt on a hedgehog.

'**Go away!**' he shouted, half out of fright, half out of anger.

'I've come to read the gas meter,' said a voice on the other side of the door. Mr Quire sighed:

'Oh very well. Come in if you must.'

Mr Quire showed the gasman where the meter was and went into his drawing room. He was already beginning to feel nervous about the audition this evening and began pacing up and down the carpet. He decided he would practise some lines from the play, just to make sure he hadn't forgotten any. He lay down on his settee with the back of his hand resting on his forehead and prepared to deliver Sir John's opening speech from the first scene of the play.

(Sir John Tressillie is standing gazing up at a portrait of his young wife and son. They have been kidnapped by smugglers some time ago and each year, on the anniversary of their disappearance, Sir John unveils the painting.)

Sir John (very dramatically) Oh Fateful day! Oh Day of Woe and Misery! Once again, my eyes filled with tears must turn in remembrance to that Image of my Saintly Wife and lost, lost Boy. Kidnapped, worse than dead! Ah when will my poor, torn Heart cease to remember you? Must I live, live on in despair? Oh cruel, cruel Fate!

(*Enter the Gasman. He sees this man lying on the settee, moaning and wailing. He can't make out what he's saying, except for the last bit about 'Cruel, cruel feet!'*)

Gasman

> I know how you feel, mate! Blimey, the trouble I have with my feet! They play me up something wicked! Mind you, it's not surprising doing this job. Do you know how many miles I walk a week? You wouldn't believe how many miles I walk a week. And the number of pairs of shoes I get through! I have to go to the chiropodist once a month. It all costs money, you know. And the Gas Board doesn't pay for it, oh no!

Sir John (*sitting up, astonished and irritated by this interruption*)

> It is quite extraordinary. I have never met you before in my Life. I do not know you from Adam. And yet, you feel you can just stand there and prrrrattle on about your feet! Your feet do not interest *me* in the slightest, my man. You have interrupted me in the middle of preparing for this crucial audition. What are you trying to do? Ruin my career? I suggest you leave *immediately*.

Gasman (*annoyed at being talked to in this way*)

> Be like that then. That's all the thanks I get for being concerned, is it? I hope you get varookas, you windbag!

Sir John (*furious*) WINDBAG! WIIINDBAG! You, Sir, are the Windbag. You obviously do not know who you are talking to! (*Exit the Gasman*) None other than the GRRRRREAT . . .

But it was too late. Mr Quire heard the front door slam. He lay down on his settee again, almost beside himself with rage and frustration. He tried to pick up the thread of his speech, but he couldn't remember where he'd got to. So he went on to his favourite scene. Near the end of the play, Sir John comes face to face with the leader of the smugglers who had kidnapped his wife and child. Norbert Quire cleared his throat, narrowed his eyes and cried out:

'You Damned Scoundrel! Black-hearted **villain!** Despicable Wretch! I loathe and despise you. I fear not your threats and menaces, Knave. Back, back I say, and learn to respect that which you have **daaaaaaared** to trifle with—a Woman's honour and her . . . .'

BRRRBRRR . . . . . brrrbrrr . . . . . BRRRBRRR . . . . brrrbrrr . . .

Mr Quire sighed deeply:

'I do not believe it!' he said. 'The World is against me. I shall go for a walk. I must get some air.'

In the hallway he crammed his hat down onto his head, pulled on his coat and wrapped two scarves around his neck. He left the flat with the telephone still ringing in the drawing room.

Out in the street, Mr Quire took a deep breath in order to calm himself down. As the cold air touched his lungs it made him cough and further irritated his sore throat. He set off down the street, slouching through the press of morning shoppers, so wrapped up in his thoughts and two scarves that he barely noticed their presence as they passed by to the left and right of him. He had not gone very far, however, when he suddenly stopped short in the middle of the pavement, stood quite still and listened. He had caught the sound of a clock in the distance chiming the hour.

'The Bells, the Bells,' muttered Norbert Quire in a deep, dark voice. He gave a little shiver. It may have been the cold, or it may have been the memory of his last play that made Mr Quire shiver. Even now the newspaper report was still fresh in his mind.

THE HUNCHBACK OF NOTRE DAME

The title role of Quasimodo was played by Mr Norbert Quire. His performance as the tragic bellringer was perhaps over-enthusiastic. He hobbled and snarled around the stage, eyes flashing and talking in such a booming voice that he could probably have been heard in the street. The best moment in the play came in the middle of the second act. At this point, the hump that had been on Mr Quire's shoulder slid down the front of his tunic and came to rest on his stomach. He may have begun the play as Quasimodo, but he ended it looking like Bessie Bunter. I have not laughed so much in a long time.

For an actor as serious as Mr Quire, this performance had been a nightmare. This was why he was so eager to get the part of Sir John Tressillie—to restore his dented reputation.

Mr Quire walked on through the foggy streets. The only thing that distracted him during his wanderings was a flower shop. He stopped to look at the display of colour which stood out so brilliantly against the gloom of this winter's day.

'Ah, can Spring be far away?' Mr Quire sighed. 'Oh to be in fields of scarlet poppies, or down among the water meadows where the cowslips blow.' He decided to buy another potted plant to cheer himself up.

When Mr Quire left the flower shop half an hour later, he was carrying a large, brightly coloured, strongly scented potted plant under his arm. Rather than returning to his flat straight away he thought he might continue his walk beside the river for a while. To reach the river he had to cross the road, and having looked both ways, Mr Quire stepped out. Suddenly a van loomed out of the fog. It was heading straight for him. It hadn't seen him. With great exertion, Norbert Quire launched himself and his plant towards the far pavement and somehow managed to reach it just as the van flashed past him, horn blaring, and disappeared into the fog again. Mr Quire stood for a moment on the grassy verge hugging his plant and composing himself. The sudden effort, the cold air and the fright all combined to make him cough and cough and cough.

Mr Quire picked up his hat from where it had fallen and made his way along the embankment beside the river. He wandered up and down for a long while. Now and then he would stop and lean over the low stone wall, looking down into the sluggish waters of the river. The far bank was almost entirely hidden in the shifting mist. The only sound that he could hear was the muffled drone of the traffic behind him and, out there on the river, the doleful voices of the barges and tugboats calling to one another.

Norbert Quire returned to his flat with a heavy tread. He sat in his drawing room still wearing his hat, coat and two scarves and still holding his potted plant. His walk had done him more harm than good. He was feeling weak and dejected. His throat was inflamed and sore. But the quiet of the flat pleased him.

BRRRBRRR . . . . . brrrbrrr . . . . . BRRRBRRR . . . . .
. . . brrrbrrr . . . . . BRRRBRRR . . . . .

Mr Quire rose out of his armchair and went to answer the phone. He removed both the scarves from round his mouth.

'Hello . . . . Hello . . . . . . Norbert, are you there?'

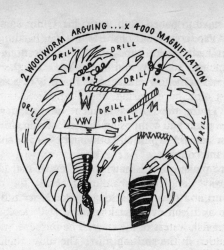

2. WOODWORM ARGUING ... X 4000 MAGNIFICATION

Chapter 7

As George was driving home from the Lost Voice Office with his daughter, his mood picked up a bit and he felt more jovial. It was probably the thought of food that prompted this. But also he was just pleased to be out of that place. Apart from having been bored, he had felt very uneasy sitting there with all those silent people. It was creepy. He had hardly dared speak himself and from time to time he needed to whisper something to Alfreda, just to make sure that his own voice was still there. He was certainly glad that Alfreda's voice had been handed in so promptly. He didn't want to spend any more time in that place than was absolutely necessary. And, yes, he had to admit it had been a bit cruel of him to suggest that they wait till next year before visiting the Lost Voice Office. He looked across at his daughter sitting in the passenger seat. Alfreda was all right. Some of her jokes even made him laugh from time to time. He smiled at her and, for a moment, it almost seemed to George as if she had a serious expression on her face. Alfreda! Serious! That'll be the day! he thought.

As George was locking the car, Alfreda strode in the front door and promptly fell over the satchel she'd left there earlier.

'Damn and Blast!' she boomed. 'Damn fool place to put a satchel!'

Alfreda sat on the floor rubbing her knee and wondering why she'd come out with such a funny-sounding expression. At the same moment, Marjorie came out of the kitchen wiping her hands on a red and white check tea towel.

'I seem to remember asking you to move that before you left,' she said.

'Good evening, Mother,' said Alfreda, picking herself up. Marjorie looked at her daughter suspiciously.

'Successful?' she asked.

'Yes,' replied George, shutting the door behind him. 'Someone had handed it in.'

Marjorie bent down and put her arm around Alfreda's shoulder.

'You still sound a bit rough to me. But then, that's hardly surprising. You haven't shaken off your cold or your sore throat yet. It's no wonder you sound a bit hoarse. I think the best thing for you would be something to eat, then straight up to bed with a hot drink.'

'Very well, Mother. If you insist,' agreed Alfreda in a surprisingly deep and resonant voice.

George suddenly looked concerned. He too bent down towards Alfreda. Unless he was very much mistaken, or unless his ears were deceiving him, he had just heard Alfreda not only agree with her mother, but agree to go to bed early!

'Are you sure you're feeling all right?' he asked.

'I assure you I am fine,' Alfreda barked.

'Only asking,' George replied. 'And there's no need to get stroppy with me!'

The evening meal was eaten in silence, which was something of a rare occurrence in the Abbot household, and at the end, as George was taking the plates out, Marjorie asked Alfreda what she would like to drink. Marjorie then followed George into the kitchen and began searching around in the shelves.

'What are you looking for?' asked George.

'Camomile tea,' Marjorie replied. 'Alfreda asked for camomile tea.'

'What! Who put that idea into her head?'

'I don't know. Some sort of food fad she's brought home from school I expect.'

'Honestly!' sighed George. 'When I was her age we drank what we were given. None of this camomile tea nonsense.'

'There's something not quite right with that girl,' Marjorie whispered to her husband. 'I don't know what it is, but she sounds . . . . . different.'

'Don't be silly,' replied George. 'You said yourself that she's got a cold. We all sound different when we've got colds.'

At that moment Alfreda appeared in the kitchen and Marjorie quickly had to explain that there didn't seem to be any camomile tea.

'I can buy some tomorrow on my way home from work,' she suggested.

'If you wish,' replied Alfreda. 'But, to tell you the truth, it is *filthy* stuff. I don't know why I drink it. *I* wouldn't give it to a dog myself.'

Alfreda settled for a glass of hot milk and when she received it she said simply:

'Thank you, Mother. I shall retire to my bed now. Goodnight Mother. Goodnight Father. Goodnight. Goodnight.'

And with that, she went upstairs.

Reg was on the landing at this time. Just outside the bathroom, he had one ear pressed against the skirting board and was listening to two woodworm arguing. He heard Alfreda coming up the stairs before he saw her. She was making these little coughing noises—ahem, ahem—as if she had something stuck in her throat that she couldn't get rid of.

'Hello,' he said as she reached the top step.

'Good evening, Reginald.'

Reg raised one eyebrow in surprise and asked:

'Where are you off to then?'

'I am off to the Kingdom of Dreams,' came the deep and dark reply.

'On the Wings of Sleep.'

'Good. Fine. Have a nice trip.'

Reg watched Alfreda disappear into her bedroom, and as he did so he thought:

'What very strange behaviour!'

Then he shrugged his shoulders and pressed his ear once more to the skirting board eager to find out which of the two woodworm was winning the argument.

Chapter 8

When Norbert Quire recovered from his faint, he found himself lying on the floor still clutching the dead telephone in his hand. He looked at his watch. It said 6.35. He had an hour and twenty-five minutes to get his voice back and make it to the audition. He rushed out of the house and caught a bus to the town centre, although it took him ten minutes to explain to the bus conductor where he wanted to go. When he reached the Town Hall, he ran up the wide staircase, through the elaborate arch and into the Lost Voice Office.

His heart sank when he saw the number of people in the room. He almost decided to give up there and then. But he stayed. He waited for what seemed like an eternity and as each moment passed, the tension of waiting got worse until he thought he could no longer bear it. And this wasn't helped by a horrid little girl in front of him who kept turning round and staring or grinning at him.

When his number was finally called out, Norbert dared to look at his watch. Yes, he still had time, if he hurried. He filled in his form and handed over his birth certificate. The man behind the counter disappeared into the rows of shelves once again. Norbert waited. He shifted from foot to foot. More waiting. The man reappeared holding nothing more than the pieces of paper.

'Sorry, Mr Squire, I can't find your voice anywhere. If you only lost it today it may not have been handed in yet. Try again tomorrow.'

The man called out another number and looked over Norbert's shoulder to see who was next. Norbert clenched his fist and began jumping up and down on the spot. This little dance was so full of fury and frustration he seemed in danger of exploding. The man behind the counter was not amused.

'Look, if your voice isn't here, it isn't here. There's nothing I can do about it. You'll just have to be patient.'

Norbert tore the papers from the man's hand and jabbed his finger against the top line pointing to where his name had been written. The Lost Voice Man looked first very angry, then confused. Norbert took out a pen and drew a large full stop between the 'S' and the 'Q' of his name. Then he pointed at it again with a desperate look on his face.

'Oh I see,' said the man behind the counter, 'it's Quire, not Squire. Hang on a mo, I'll go and have another look.'

'Sorry about that,' said the man as he returned with Norbert's voice and ripped open the plastic package. A look of relief was written all over the actor's face. He took his snowflake of a voice and, placing it on his tongue, he set out for the audition.

It was on the bus, en route to the theatre, that Norbert had the first opportunity to try out his voice. He was concerned that it might have got damaged in some way. The person who found it might have handled it roughly, or it may have got knocked about at the Lost Voice Office, although voices are very resilient. They can survive the harshest of conditions. When the conductor asked for his fare, he replied:

'Thirty p.'

Norbert was a little startled by this. The sound that came out of his mouth was rather high-pitched. It certainly was not the rich, mellow tone he had expected. Still, it always takes a while for a voice to settle back in. The Lost Voice Man had said it would be half an hour or so before it was absolutely right. That would give Norbert time enough before he was due to do his audition.

When Mr Quire arrived at the theatre he went backstage and stood in the darkness of the wings with his fellow actors. The butterflies he'd felt earlier came back worse than ever, but to the outside world he appeared calm and confident. Many of the other actors were still rehearsing their lines, either silently or in whispers, making exaggerated dumb-show gestures to nobody in particular. It was rather like being in the middle of an orchestra tuning up. Mr Quire recognised some of them from other auditions. They exchanged nods and glances, but no words. Only one of them came up to him as he stood with his arms crossed and his nose in the air.

'Forgotten your script, Norbert?' he asked. 'Sorry, but I'm not lending you mine.'

Mr Quire turned away and ignored this intrusion. His memory was so formidable *he* didn't need a script.

After ten minutes or so, Mr Quire's name was called out. Norbert stepped out of the darkness onto the brightly lit stage. He stood for a while blinking in the glare of the spotlights, but when his eyes got used to the light, he could just make out the rows of empty seats in front of him, and the solitary, dark figure of the director sitting in the midst of them. He addressed Norbert:

'O.K. Mr Quire. Now, I want you to do the first scene from the play. Remember, Sir John is looking up at the portrait of his wife and son. He is grief-stricken, inconsolable. I want plenty of feeling, lots of emotion. Off you go.'

The big moment had come at last. Mr Quire spent a few moments composing himself, calming himself down. He cleared his throat, adopted an expression of great sadness and began:

'I eat my dog with relish, I like the taste a lot . . . .'

Mr Quire suddenly swung round to find out where this silly voice was coming from. It sounded like a young girl. For some reason she was trying to put him off, to spoil his chances. Undaunted, he carried on:

'A sausage dog is good when cold . . . .'

What!!! There it was again. He looked about him, furious. In the wings, the other actors were either laughing or sniggering or standing with a look of complete astonishment on their faces.

'I'm sorry, I didn't quite catch that, Mr Quire,' said the Director from the auditorium.

'A sausage dog is good when cold. It's even better . . . hot.'

The awful truth suddenly struck Norbert Quire. *He* was the one reciting this silly poem. The voice was coming out of *his* mouth. He stood in the spotlights looking dumbfounded and a sense of panic began to rise in him. The director's voice was heard from the darkness again:

'Thank you, Mr Quire. I don't think we need to hear any more. It's obvious you had no intention of taking this audition seriously. Frankly I don't know why you bothered coming at all. Perhaps you think it's funny wasting everybody's time like this. Next one, please.'

'Now hang on a minute, mate . . .' Norbert piped up.

'That will be all, Mr Quire.'

Norbert had clapped his hand over his own mouth to stop anything else coming out. He couldn't believe it. 'Mate' !!?? He'd never called anybody 'Mate' in his life!

With his hand still over his mouth, Norbert Quire slowly left the stage. As he approached the wings the sound of laughter began to ring in his ears. He had to run the gauntlet of the other actors who gathered round as he came off. Some were simply laughing at Norbert's misfortune:

'Brilliant performance, Norbert, old man. Very moving, very moving.'

Others genuinely thought this was the funniest thing they'd heard for a long time:

'How did you do that voice, Norbert? It sounded so convincing!'

Norbert Quire didn't stop. He kept walking towards the stage door, his hand still clamped firmly over his mouth. He looked like a man walking to his own execution. As he was about to leave by the stage door, a man in a well-cut black coat that was far too large caught up with him.

'I don't think you got the part, old son,' said the man with a grin.

'You wouldn't have been right for it anyway. Ever tried any comedy? You should have heard the blokes back here during your performance! Killing themselves laughing they were. One of your own poems was it?'

'Mmmmmmmmmm,' replied Norbert through his hand.

The man took this to mean 'yes'.

'And the little girl's voice, that was very clever. Do you do any other impressions?'

'Mmmmmmmmmm,' replied Norbert.

'Good,' said the man with a smile. 'I think I could probably get some work for you. It won't be anything much, but it'll be better than nothing. My name's Monty Banks, by the way. Here's my card.'

Monty Banks slipped his business card into the top pocket of Mr Quire's jacket and slapped him on the back. Norbert hurried off.

Once outside the theatre, Norbert checked to see if anyone was about. When he'd made sure the street was deserted, he slowly peeled back his hand from his mouth and breathed in a great lungfull of air. Then he let it all out in a huge sigh. He didn't take the bus home. Instead he just walked, walked at random, not knowing where he was going. Two hours later he found himself standing in the hallway to his flat. He was feeling so tired and confused he couldn't even begin to make sense of what had happened.

If you want my opinion, I think it's quite astonishing that in this day and age such a mix-up could take place. That two people as different as Norbert and Alfreda could end up with each other's voices is nothing short of a scandal. You can easily imagine such a thing happening in the old days before the Lost Voice Office became automated, when they didn't have all the sophisticated machines they have today. You can understand a mistake like this happening then. Indeed, at that time, I suspect there were a whole lot of people wandering around with the wrong voice. But today there is just no excuse for it!

The question is are we simply going to accept this situation, sit on our backsides and do nothing, hoping that everything will be sorted out in the end? Or are we going to do something positive about this mess?

Like what? I hear you ask. Well, the first thing we can do is go down to the Lost Voice Office and talk to the man in charge. We can present him with all the facts and ask him how a mistake like this could have occurred. The problem is that he would probably deny that anything has gone wrong. And even if it had he would probably say:

'It's not my fault. I followed all the correct procedures which are specially laid down to prevent this sort of error from taking place. And if you're not satisfied, then I suggest you go and see the manager of the Complaints Department. If you go out of this door turn right, down to the end of the corridor, turn right again, his office is the fourth on the left. You'll see the sign on the door.'

So we follow the man's instructions and find ourselves standing outside the door of the Complaints Department. After knocking on the door we go in, only to be told by the manager, sitting behind his desk:

'Look, I'm sorry, but I'm extremely busy at the moment. Is there any chance of your coming back tomorrow?'

Well, I don't know about you, but I really don't think I can spare the time tomorrow. So the only thing to do is to sit and wait until the manager can see us. We have to sit on those uncomfortable chairs and read old magazines until he finally finds the time to listen to our questions. And when he does he goes into this long, detailed and very boring explanation all about how voices are identified, catalogued and stored. He ends by saying:

'All of this proves conclusively that it is utterly impossible for two voices to get mixed up.'

And you don't look like you understand this any better than I do. But there's nothing more we can do. So we thank him and leave. And I'm sorry I dragged you along here in the first place.

Chapter 9

Jenny Barnett strode briskly into her classroom, said good morning to her pupils and sat down at her desk. She was in a no-nonsense mood today, keen to get things done, and expected the same from her class.

'Right,' she said. 'Let's go through the homework you did last night. The answer to question . . . . Alfreda, why haven't you got your book open?'

She had looked up to see Alfreda sitting at her desk with her arms folded, glancing around the room.

'Have you done your homework?' the teacher asked.

'I am afraid not,' replied Alfreda in such a booming voice that April, sitting next to her, nearly fell off her chair. Everybody in the class turned round and stared at her. Some sniggered. Others, including Parkway, simply looked in astonishment. Alfreda sat there covered in embarrassment and confusion at the way she had replied.

'Why are you talking in that ridiculous way?' asked Ms Barnett.

'I have a cold,' Alfreda said quickly in the same deep tone.

'I see. Well, why haven't you done any homework?'

The answer was delivered in a slow and pompous manner.

'I had a rather important engagement actually.'

Ms Barnett was beginning to get irritated with Alfreda.

'Oh really! An important engagement, eh! What was it? Another meeting with the Prime Minister?'

'It was a private matter. Of concern to nobody but myself.'

Jenny Barnett had had about enough of this.

'Alfreda, I'm fed up with your silly excuses. You've tried this on once too often. It's about time you . . .'

'There is no need for you to raise your voice like that. I am not **deaf**,' Alfreda interrupted.

There were one or two gasps from the class and Ms Barnett was left dumbfounded, at a loss for words. Alfreda, when she saw her speechless, mouth gaping open like a fish, decided that this might be a good opportunity to say a little more, to see how far she could go.

'Madam, I really cannot understand why you are getting quite so upset about this rather trivial matter. I have simply failed to complete a piece of homework, that is all. It is not the End of the World, is it?'

Jenny Barnett, mouth still agape, shook her head.

'It's not the End of Civilisation as we know it, is it?'

She shook her head again.

'No, of course not,' Alfreda continued. 'There are more important things in Life than homework, Dear Lady. Grrrreat Drama, for example! However, as you obviously attach such importance to it, I shall, in future, endeavour to carry out any task you may set.'

At this point, Eddie Jennings decided to join in.

'What are you rabbiting on about, Abbot? Why don't you shut up!'

Alfreda, on hearing this, half rose out of her seat, fixed Eddie with a steely gaze, and in a thunderous voice that made the windows rattle and the welkin ring, she boomed:

'How daaaare you talk to me like that, you ill-mannered oaf! You insolent Buffoon!'

Parkway put his hands over his ears so he wouldn't have to hear any more of what Alfreda was saying. She must be mad, talking like that, to Eddie Jennings of all people! Alfreda, on the other hand, was still staring at Eddie. At first she thought she must be mistaken. But no, it was definitely there, on Eddie's face, a look of sheer terror. Alfreda had frightened the living daylights out of him with this voice and if she could frighten Eddie Jennings with it, who knew what she couldn't do. The embarrassment and confusion evaporated as Alfreda decided that she was really enjoying herself, and quite frankly, she had no intention of stopping there:

'It's about time you learnt some Manners, young man. You sit there like some Overblown **wiiiindbag** telling others what to do! Well, I for one will not stand for it! I think I have made myself clear.' And with that, Alfreda sat down again, looking rather pleased with herself. Silence reigned in the classroom for a full minute before Ms Barnett, flustered and bemused, stammered:

'Right . . . . er . . . now, where were we? Ah yes! Question one. Does anybody know the answer to question one?'

Parkway was paying no attention to Ms Barnett. He was still staring at Alfreda, sitting there with that air of self-satisfaction.

'What's she up to?' he wondered.

It wasn't until breaktime that he got the opportunity to talk to her. He spotted her wandering around the playground with her hands behind her back looking up at the clouds and apparently unaware of all the noise and commotion going on around her.

'Alf!' Parkway called.

'Ah, there you are, dear boy! I have been looking for you.'

Alfreda and Parkway walked on a way together. Then Parkway asked:

'What are you playing at, Alfreda? Why are you going around sounding like my old Grandad?'

'I am a little hoarse,' she snapped.

Parkway burst out laughing, even if it was an old joke. But his laughter didn't last long as he noticed Eddie and two of his friends coming across the playground towards them.

'Oh no!' he said with a hint of panic in his voice. He wasn't sure whether to stand in front of Alfreda or behind her, so he ended up doing this little hopping dance around her. Even Alfreda with her nose in the air couldn't help noticing Parkway's antics.

'What on earth are you doing, dear boy. Sometimes your behaviour can be quite ridiculous.'

'It's Eddie . . . coming to have a word with us . . you.'

'How tiresome,' Alfreda said and she continued scanning the clouds without even looking at the approaching menace.

Although the *idea* of protecting Alfreda appealed to Parkway, in reality he knew he wasn't big enough or strong enough for any heroics. So he took up a position to one side of and just behind Alfreda and stood there hoping she wouldn't say anything stupid that might upset Eddie. That way the two of them might escape without any damage being done. Eddie Jennings stopped in front of the two friends and looked threatening.

'You think you're bloody clever, Abbot,' he began. 'Think you're funny too, don't you? Well, I don't, see! In fact, you get up my nose!'

'Yeah,' said one of Eddie's mates.

But before he had a chance to continue, Alfreda, in a deeply bored voice, said:

'Parkway, I detect a rather unpleasant smell all of a sudden. Do you know what it might be?'

Parkway gulped and laughed nervously.

'Just a little joke, Eddie. She doesn't really mean it.'

'Shut your gob, squirt. I'm warning you, Abbot. Next time I'll . . .'

'Go away!' barked Alfreda, and Eddie leapt backwards like he'd got an electric shock.

'Right! That's it! I warned you! You're for it now!' he spluttered.

'Yeah!' said one of his mates and the three of them walked off mumbling threats. Alfreda looked completely unconcerned. She merely remarked to Parkway how poetic the clouds were looking today, and he, whose heart was still beating rather quickly, replied:

'I think you're off your head.'

Over the next few weeks it wouldn't only be Parkway who thought Alfreda had a screw loose. April even tried to find somebody who'd swap desks with her. On the other hand there were many who didn't notice any change in Alfreda, or else didn't realise she was behaving any differently from usual. The headmaster, for instance. He was sitting in his office on a bright spring morning, and had just finished sharpening all his pencils to a very fine point, when there came a knock on his door. He said come in and standing in the doorway was a young girl, probably in first year. He vaguely recognised her face, but couldn't put a name to it. He was on the point of asking in his kindly, headmaster way what the little girl wanted, but he didn't get the chance, as this booming voice addressed him:

'I am sorry to disturb you, Headmaster. I can see you're a busy man. However, I really must protest. I am being treated like a child! Things have become quite intolerable. It seems I cannot open my mouth, no word can fall from my lips, without someone getting upset.'

The small girl stopped and waited for some sort of response from the headmaster, but he was so taken aback by this opening speech that he didn't know what to say.

'Er . . . . . well . . . er . . . . well, now . . . . perhaps we should begin at the beginning. Yes. Now, who was it sent you here?'

'I was sent to you by one Mrs Griffiths, a teacher of Science. I take it you know the woman concerned.'

'Oh yes, yes. I know Mrs Griffiths.'

'Good. This morning she was explaining to the class about flowers. More particularly, about how flowers . . . . .'

Alfreda hesitated. A hint of embarrassment had crept into her voice.

'. . . . how they make other flowers . . . pollination, I think it is called. Headmaster, did you know this sort of thing was being taught in your school?'

'Yes.'

'And you approve?'

'Er, I . .'

'Well I do not,' Alfreda said emphatically. 'In fact I find it all rather disgusting and frankly I'm surprised that a man like you allows this sort of thing to go on.'

Alfreda leant forward on the headmaster's desk and her voice took on a sort of beseeching tone.

'Flowers are such delicate objects,' she continued. 'Things of Beauty, the Stuff of Poetry, a splash of Colour amid Life's Greyness, not something to be pulled apart and prodded.'

'I suppose you have a point there,' the headmaster conceded. 'But . .'

'Precisely. And I made this point to that Griffiths woman, who took no notice of me. So to illustrate my point further I began reciting for the benefit of the class, one of my favourite poems which contains the following lines:

> From every gentle flower's lip,
> The honey bee is wont to sip,
> The luscious, golden liquid,
> And carry it without a drip,
> Home to the hive for tea.'

'That's a very fine poem,' said the headmaster with a beaming smile.

'Thank you. Unfortunately Mrs Griffiths did not find it so. She accused me of fooling around. **Fooling around!** I ask you! It's outrageous.'

Here Alfreda's deep dark voice took on such a sombre, pitiful tone that it almost brought tears to the headmaster's eyes.

'Here I am, trying to bring a little Poetry, a little Beauty, into the lives of others, Headmaster, and I am accused of fooling around. My reward is to be punished for it. Where is the Justice in that?'

'Most unjust!' said the headmaster, sternly.

'The question is, then, what are you going to do about it? Is this Griffiths woman going to be allowed to continue teaching in this way, exposing young minds to such ideas?'

'Well, the problem is, I can't tell Mrs Griffiths on my own what she should teach . . .'

'Good God, man, do you run this school or not?'

'Oh yes, yes I do. It's just that I have to ask a lot of other people what they think before any changes can be made. I suggest you leave the problem with me and I'll get back to you after I've spoken to those concerned.'

Alfreda sighed with impatience.

'Oh very well. Perhaps we can continue this discussion at a later date.'

'Certainly.' The headmaster got out of his chair and shook Alfreda by the hand. Then he showed her to the door, saying:

'It's been a great pleasure talking to you. A most fruitful discussion, sir. And as I say, you will be hearing from me as soon as possible.' He showed Alfreda out and was returning to his desk, when it suddenly dawned on him. He'd spent the last quarter of an hour being told how to do his job—by a first form girl!

'She can't do that!' he said and ran to the door. 'Oi, you come back here!' he called out.

But the corridor was empty.

Going home on the bus that evening, Alfreda recounted the events that had taken place in the headmaster's office.

' 'Course you did,' said Sheila with a sneer, not believing one word of what Alfreda had said.

'Are you calling me a Liar?' said Alfreda aggressively. Sheila backed down and decided that Alfreda was becoming a bit too bossy all of a sudden.

'Did he really shake your hand?' asked April.

'Indeed he did, but to tell the truth, I found the man to be a complete and utter fool.'

The conversation then turned to the subject of the school disco at the end of term. Parkway said he wasn't going because he couldn't dance and no amount of persuasion would make him change his mind. Alfreda didn't want to go either, but Sheila and April kept on at her.

'Oh come on, Alfreda. It'll be fun.'

'Anyway, I thought you liked dancing,' said April.

'Ah Dancing, Dancing!' said Alfreda, staring at nothing in particular. 'The elegance of the Waltz, a dashing two-step! Alas, no. My dancing days are over.'

'Oh don't be so stupid. Blimey, nobody'll want to dance with you if you talk like that!'

Finally, Alfreda was persuaded to go. On the evening of the dance she arrived with her two friends. The school hall had been decked out with flashing, bright lights and posters such that it looked just like a school hall decked out with lights and posters. The three girls sat down on the chairs that had been set out around the edge of the hall. Up on the stage at the far end, surrounded by speakers and more flashing lights, stood a bored-looking disc jockey. Music blared out across the room.

'Good, innit!' said Sheila enthusiastically.

Alfreda raised her eyebrows and tutted. She watched groups of friends standing around who were watching other groups of friends or who were watching the dancers who were watching each other or staring at their feet. All in all there was a lot of watching going on.

After a while Alfreda was deserted by her two friends who had gone off to join another group huddled in one corner. She carried on watching the dancers, although at the same time she did notice a boy who had been slowly and casually making his way towards her. Eventually he sat down on a chair next to her, but he acted as if she wasn't really there. Alfreda looked at him out of the corner of her eye. He sat there for quite a while, occasionally waving to somebody across the room. But most of the time he had his arms crossed and was tapping his foot in time with the music. Finally he plucked up the courage to speak to Alfreda.

'You're in first year, aren't you?'

Alfreda looked down her nose at him and said nothing. A bit later he added:

'I'm in third year.'

There was another long pause during which time he went back to tapping his foot and watching the dancers. Then:

'My name's Dave.'

Alfreda turned away and tutted. Even so, Dave was really enjoying himself. He had never been very good at talking to girls he didn't know and this was his most successful conversation so far. As far as he was concerned it was all going swimmingly. He was beginning to feel quite relaxed. This was all much easier than he thought it would be. By now he was leaning back in his chair with his hands behind his head.

'What's your name?' he asked.

Alfreda did not bother to turn round and pretended not to hear the question. At this point Dave started shifting about in his chair, holding onto the edges. It was obvious he was working up to something, which finally and nervously he managed to say:

'You want a dance?'

Alfreda turned round slowly and looked at Dave. Then her voice boomed out above the music:

'Young man, you come and sit down next to me without so much as a by your leave. I do not know you from Adam, nor do I wish to. We have not as far as I am aware, been introduced, and yet you have the audacity to ask me to dance. You ought to be thoroughly ashamed of yourself. I am deeply shocked.'

Alfreda was not half as shocked as Dave who sat there for a moment, stunned. Then he rushed off. Alfreda was not troubled by anybody else asking her to dance that evening.

When George arrived to pick up his daughter later on, he found her sitting by herself in an almost empty hall. The flashing lights had been turned off and the neon tubes which lit the place gave off a harsh glare. Alfreda stood up when she saw her father arrive and the two of them walked to the car.

'Enjoy yourself?' asked George.

'Not to my taste, Father. I feel the evening would have been better spent at the Theatre.'

'Well, I can't disagree with you there,' said George which was strange, because it was probably the first time that Alfreda and George had agreed about anything.

Norbert Quire, meanwhile . . . . ?

Chapter 10

'What d'you get if you cross a pig with a telephone?'

Norbert Quire suddenly sat bolt upright in bed and heard himself ask this riddle. That voice again!!! It danced around the bedroom in the darkness, making Mr Quire shudder. Then he slumped back into his pillows, confused and bewildered. Something very strange had happened. It was as if his own voice had shattered into a thousand tinkling pieces. And not only had it gone all high-pitched, but it had gathered up from somewhere a flock of silly rhymes and jokes, riddles, puns and absurd stories. These kept popping into Norbert's head unbidden, where they would wheel and circle like demented birds.

It was another week before Norbert Quire felt strong enough to get out of bed. He sat in his dressing gown in his drawing room all day long trying to decide what to do next. He was still haunted by the memories of the audition. The laughter of his fellow actors kept ringing in his ears, turning even his waking hours into a nightmare. And yet, the only thing that concerned him was how he was going to get back on the stage. It became an obsession. Like a criminal who wants to return to the scene of his crime, Mr Quire was desperate to perform again, he longed to be seen again, to receive that thunderous applause again. There was a knock on the door, but Norbert ignored it.

The problem was how could he possibly get *knockknock* . . . the problem was how could he possibly get back on the stage when *knockknock* . . . how could he possibly get back on the stage when his voice was *knockknock* . . . when his voice was *knockknock* . . . the problem was how could he possibly *knockknock* . . . the possem was probably how he could stage a setback *knockknock* . . .

Norbert's rage at this insistent knocking grew until his patience finally snapped. He rushed into the hallway:

'Look, **bog off, will you!**' he piped.

Norbert clapped his hand over his mouth in shock. There was a pause followed by another couple of knocks, then a woman's voice said:

'Let me in. I want to see Mr Quire.'

'Oh blimey!' said Norbert under his breath when he recognised the voice. Then louder: 'He's not here. Mr Quire's gone away. And he told me not to let anybody in.'

Another pause.

'Well, when he gets back you can tell him Deirdre called round. You can also tell him I think you're a very rude little girl, whoever you are!'

Norbert listened to the sound of footsteps receding into the distance and the front door being shut firmly. 'Sorry, Deirdre,' he said. Then he shuffled slowly back to his drawing room. Return to the stage? It was pointless. How could he deliver those profoundly tragic lines with such a high-pitched voice? Who would take him seriously? He may as well face it. He'd never perform again. For four days he wandered around his flat as if he was wandering through the ruins of his career.

It was only on the fifth day, when Norbert had finally decided to get dressed, that he came across the card as he was putting on his jacket. He turned the small white rectangle in his hand and read what was printed on it.

MONTGOMERY BANKS
*Theatrical impresario
and agent*

Norbert suddenly remembered. At the audition. Yeah. A small bloke. Big coat. What had he said? 'I could get some work for you, old son.' Norbert looked at the card again. Perhaps this Mr Banks could help. Why not? After all he had nothing to lose.

Several days later Norbert Quire was sitting in a dingy outer office waiting for Montgomery Banks to see him. The walls of this outer office were lined with photographs of all the acts that Mr Banks managed. There was a photo of a magician wearing a black tailcoat passing a large hoop around the body of a young woman floating horizontally three feet above the stage. He had a thin, pointed beard and a curled moustache. His left arm was raised triumphantly. Next to this was one of a woman ventriloquist with a sad-looking dummy sitting on her knee. Above this, one of a man leading a procession of dogs who walked on their hind legs and carried umbrellas. It was this one that Norbert was examining when Mr Banks appeared.

'Good to see you, Norbert, old son. Come on in.'

Norbert followed Mr Banks into his office and sat down.

'Nice place you got here, Monty,' said Norbert, looking around. 'I like the dogs with umbrellas.'

Monty Banks started laughing.

'Sorry, Norbert. It's that voice. It cracks me up.'

'Oh yeah,' piped Norbert, po-faced.

'I've been telling everybody I meet about your peformance at the audition. Funniest thing I've seen for a long time. The director was still steaming mad an hour later. Anyway, the thing is how can we find you some work? What are you going to do?'

'Dunno,' Norbert said. 'I've got these.' He pulled out of his pocket a wad of paper. During his idle moments, and to take his mind off his sorry state of affairs, he had copied down many of the poems and stories that had filled his head. There was page after page of nonsense of all sorts; a poem about a talking dog, another about being attacked by a giant bowl of spaghetti, a story about a man who stands in front of the mirror with his eyes closed to see what he looks like when he's asleep, and many more.

'What are these, then?'

'Dunno,' replied Norbert. 'Just a lot of stupid blokes doing stupid things really. Things like that.'

Monty read through some of the poems, and an idea began to form in his mind.

'Yes,' he said slowly. 'Something like . . . "The Norbert Quire One-Man Show". All you'd have to do is read out the best of these.'

Norbert shrugged his shoulders. He didn't have much confidence in the idea, or Monty Banks.

'Leave it with me, Norbert, old son. I'll be in touch.'

In the event, Norbert underestimated Monty. Within days the agent was on the phone to the actor with the funny voice telling him he had found two engagements for him, one in a community centre, the other in a school. At the appointed time and in the appointed place, Norbert arrived for the first of his recitals. The community centre hall was little more than a large room with a slightly raised stage at one end. Rows of plastic chairs had been set out and these were occupied by a handful of people, mostly elderly, some young with time on their hands.

'You sure we're in the right place?' Norbert asked Monty. 'You sure this isn't a funeral?'

Monty burst out laughing.

'That's the spirit, Norbert. Just read this lot out and make them laugh.'

Monty handed over a selection of the poems and stories and riddles that Norbert had shown him and pushed the actor towards the stage. Once on the stage, Norbert felt again the sheer thrill of performing, the sheer thrill of being in front of an audience, albeit a small one. The only bit that worried him was Monty's last words: 'Make them laugh.' He'd never made anybody laugh in his life, at least, not on purpose. He'd certainly never laughed himself. He didn't even know how to. Norbert looked at the top sheet of paper.

'Oi, wake up you lot! Here's a story. It's called the Tale of Rick and Dick Ridiculous.'

There were one or two sniggers from the audience as they listened to this piping little voice that came out of this tall, very serious-looking man standing in front of them.

'Rick and Dick Ridiculous were brothers, in fact they were identical twins. In fact they were so identical they often didn't know which one was which. One day their wives decided to play a trick on them. When Dick came home his wife said to him:

'Husband, are you ill? You're looking very pale!'

Dick, who'd never felt better in his life, said:

'If I look pale I *must* be ill. I'd better go to bed.'

Dick's friends came round to see him and agreed with his wife that he was looking unwell. One of them, who said he was a doctor, listened to his heart.

'It's getting weaker,' he pronounced gravely.

On the following day his friends returned and again stood around his bed.

'He's worse,' said one.

'He's not long for this world,' said another.

'He won't see another birthday,' said a third.

'Isn't it strange how I can feel so well, yet be so ill!' said Dick.

On the third day, the doctor announced to everybody that Dick Ridiculous had passed away. A sheet was drawn over his head.

'So this is what it's like being dead!' said Dick beneath his sheet.

Meanwhile, Rick Ridiculous was telling his wife about the very smart party he had been invited to.

'But I don't know what to wear,' he complained. 'What do fashionable people wear?'

His wife thought for a moment and then replied:

'Newspaper and dustbin lids, I think.'

'I see,' said Rick and went away to get dressed. When he reappeared he asked his wife:

'And what do they wear on their heads?'

'Cow dung,' replied his wife.

'I see,' said Rick, and he went off to make himself a hat. When he returned, his wife said:

'And you'll need a chicken on a lead. No fashionable person would be seen without a chicken on a lead.'

Rick Ridiculous clanked out of the house dragging his chicken with him. First the townspeople heard him coming, then they smelt him coming. Halfway across the town square, Rick Ridiculous met the procession that was carrying his brother, Dick, to the churchyard.

'How sad!' said Rick. 'Now Dick won't be able to see just how fashionable I am!'

When Dick saw Rick and the way he was dressed, he couldn't believe his eyes. He shouted to his brother:

'If I wasn't dead, how I would laugh at your stupidity! They've made a proper fool out of you!'

As he finished Norbert stood staring at the sheet of paper he had just been reading from. He remembered writing this out the other day sitting at his desk. But he had no idea where it had come from, any more than he understood what had happened to his voice. And it was only slowly that he became aware of the ripple of applause that sounded in the hall. He looked up rather surprised and his gaze was met by a crowd of smiling faces.

'Blimey! They must've liked it,' said the actor. He shuffled through the papers until he came across a poem. 'Right, shut up again and listen to this. It's called "The elbow that came to dinner".'

> An elbow came to dine with me.
> Its wits were sharp, its language free.
> It told me countless jokes and fibs
> And dug in to my ribs of pork.
> ('Dig in,' I said. 'Help yourself.')
> Endlessly that elbow talk-
> ed and bored me with its holiday-
> s in Elba, Greece and St Tropez.

It drank far too much strong beer
And such a huge amount of wine,
It spun around the table,
Singing 'Auld Lang Syne'.

It wouldn't go. It wouldn't leave.
I tried to kick it out.
It leapt into my coffee pot
And got stuck up the spout.

I shoved my hand into the pot,
('This elbow is a pain.')
But in the end the only thing I got
Was a nasty dark brown stain
On the tablecloth.

Then Mum's advice came back to me.
(If only I was able!)
'Whenever you are eating, dear,
Keep elbows off the table.'

By the end of the recital, some of the audience was actually laughing, although for the life of him, Norbert could not understand why. In fact, it was simply the spectacle of a man with a dead-pan face reading out a lot of nonsense in a high-pitched voice that made people laugh. Afterwards, Monty came up to Norbert and slapped him on the back.

'Not bad at all, old son,' he said.

'Better than a kick up the bum,' Norbert replied, then he put his hand over his mouth and went all bashful. 'Sorry, Monty. Didn't mean to say that.'

The first recital was followed by another at a local school where Norbert proved to be a great hit. As he was leaving, a small boy even came up and asked him for his autograph. Slowly, Norbert Quire began to make a name for himself. The audiences got bigger and Monty had to hire larger and larger places for Norbert to perform in. He had become accustomed to the strange voice that had possessed him, until now it no longer seemed strange. And still he continued to produce all manner of nonsense. Everything that happened to him gave rise to a joke or a silly poem or a barmy story.

As far as Monty Banks was concerned, Norbert was going to be a star. The two of them would meet regularly in Monty's office and he'd plan the next step.

'More publicity,' he'd say, waving his arms about in the air, 'that's what we need. A radio interview! Yes. I'll have a word with Louis. He owes me a favour.'

It was due to Monty's cousin, Louis, who worked at a local radio station that Norbert found himself, several weeks later, sitting in front of a microphone across the table from an interviewer who was just rounding off a review of the films that were on at the local cinemas:

'. . . . and this is a film I can recommend for the whole family. Now, finally on today's programme, Norbert Quire. Mr Quire has built up something of a following in this region for his recitals of poetry and the curious stories he tells. He's with us in the studio. The first thing I'd like to know, Mr Quire, is where the ideas for the poems and stories come from?'

'Dunno, really. They just sort of beep beep come out of my head.'

The interviewer looked at Norbert suspiciously.

'I see,' he continued. 'You spend a lot of your time giving recitals in schools. Do you get on well with children?'

'Nah, I think they're really beep beep boring beep.'

'Oh! Well, let's talk a bit about your voice. You seem to be . . . making these strange noises while you talk, do you always do that?'

'What beep beep noises?' asked Norbert.

'Ha, ha, ha!' the interviewer laughed nervously. 'If you don't mind my saying, you do talk in a very high-pitched voice! Have you trained yourself to do this?'

Norbert thought for a moment, scratched his head, and replied with conviction:

'Beep beep beep. Beep beebeep beep beep. Bip beep beebeep, beep beep beebeep, beebeep bip beebeep beep beep beep beep. Beep beep beep beep, bip beep beep . . .'

Meanwhile, Monty Banks was in the kitchen of his mobile home listening to all this on the radio. Halfway through opening a tin of baby carrots, he called out to his enormously fat wife, Esmerelda, who was lying on the couch:

'Turn it up a bit will you, Esme?'

Now he could clearly hear Norbert happily beeping away to himself, while in the background the interviewer was still laughing nervously and trying to get a word in edgeways. Then the laughter seemed to turn to panic and there was the sound of muttering followed by what Monty thought was the noise of a scuffle, during which Norbert let out this extra loud beep and startled the interviewer, who finally came back on the air and announced the end of the programme in a voice verging on hysterics.

Roaring with laughter, Monty switched off the radio and turned to Esmerelda lying on the couch with a huge box of chocolates.

'So,' he said all excited. 'What did you think of *that*, Esme, my dear?'

'Nougat,' she replied.

'What?'

'I can't find the nougat. I'm sure there was one left. I'll have to look on the bottom layer.'

Esmerelda rummaged around in the chocolates while Monty asked again:

'What did you think of the interview?'

'I can't see what all the fuss is about,' she replied, biting into a soft strawberry centre. 'This Norbert Whatsit. He sounds just like a big girl to me. And he talks a lot of nonsense.'

'Well, I think he's going to be a star,' said Monty defiantly.

Esmerelda was unimpressed by Monty's talk. She'd heard it all before. In fact, she'd been a star herself once. There were those who remembered her as one of the most graceful and courageous tightrope walkers in the business. Her courage was only matched by her love of chocolates, and these had proved to be her downfall.

'And that interview might be all he needs to make him a star!' Monty continued, although by now he was talking to himself.

Norbert Quire was dreading the meeting the following morning in Monty's office. He arrived like a lamb to the slaughter, his head hung low, and before Monty had a chance to say a word, the actor began in a low, apologetic voice:

'Sorry, Monty, didn't mean to do it, it was just there was this bloke, right, asking all these peabrain questions and it sort of just came out. Sorry, Monty.'

Monty put his arm around Norbert's shoulder and gave him a little hug.

'It was a stroke of genius,' he said. 'People have been phoning me all morning wanting to know about you. I've already booked four more performances. We're on our way, old son! How do you feel about that?'

Mr Quire looked at Mr Banks and said:

'Like I've been smacked in the gob, Monty.'

The two men got down to discussing plans for the future. The first project was to collect all Norbert's nonsense together in a book which would be called *A Marshmallow Writes to his Mum*. Norbert said he had just finished a short poem about teaching a sack of potatoes to dance and he was going to write another one in beep language. Norbert even suggested he could write a nonsense opera, but Monty said he was getting carried away. At the end of two hours of discussion Norbert finally got up to leave. At the door, Monty called after him:

'By the way, you don't have to put on the silly voice all the time, old son. Not with me.'

'Can't help it,' replied Norbert in the same high-pitched voice. And with a shrug of his shoulders, he left.

Later that evening, Norbert Quire was lying in his bath thinking how extraordinary all this was. All he did was beep at somebody in public and now he was going to be famous. At first he felt a flush of shame at the way he had behaved. But as he lay there conjuring up the image of the interviewer in his mind, that look of total astonishment on his face when Norbert started beeping at him, the muscles in his cheeks began to tighten. This was a wholly new experience for Norbert. And when he remembered how that look of astonishment changed to one of panic, his lips began to widen across his face. Yes, there was no doubt about it! Norbert Quire was lying in his bath, grinning. And when he got to remembering the moment when he beeped so loudly the interviewer threw his papers in the air in fright, a curious squeaking noise was formed in Norbert's throat. And when he remembered how the studio technicians had to wrestle with him to get his microphone away, this squeaky noise grew and grew until, no longer able to control it, Norbert Quire for the first time in his life, exploded into laughter. And once he had started he couldn't stop. Nor did he want to. Even as the tears rolled down his cheeks, he sent more peals of laughter ringing round the bathroom, at the same time batting the surface of the water with the flat of his hand. Anybody seeing him would have said he was behaving like a big kid.

Oh Great and Noble tree,

PARK

Chapter 11

George Abbot slopped a soapy sponge onto the bonnet of his car and pushed it round and round in a series of swirls.

'And Desmond,' he said. 'I met Desmond the other day and he said he'd never come across such a well-spoken, serious young girl as our Alfreda. "Frighteningly clever" he described her as. Quite a compliment coming from Desmond of all people. I think we have good reason to be proud of young Alfreda.'

Marjorie was standing with her arms folded, inspecting the windscreen.

'You've missed a bit. There. By the wiper.'

George, sponge in hand, swooped down on the patch of dirt and obliterated it.

'You keep going on about this, George, as if you're entirely responsible for it.'

'Oh no, I wouldn't say *that*. I couldn't take all the credit myself. But I do think if I hadn't kept on at her, she'd still be spouting all that nonsense she used to talk, all those stupid jokes and stories. It's partly because she doesn't spend nearly as much time with Harry as she used to. That's why she's begun acting more grown-up.'

Marjorie was nothing like as convinced as George that Alfreda had changed for the better, and said so.

'Now what do you mean by that?' asked George huffily.

Marjorie went on to tell him how she and Alfreda had been out shopping last Saturday when they met Mrs Peach in the High Street. Alfreda had been ever so polite and respectful to her face, but behind her back she had described her as 'a ghastly creature with the brains of a gnat'. George burst out laughing when he heard this. He picked up the bucket and threw the rest of the frothy water over the roof of the car, saying:

'I think Alfreda's absolutely right. Julia Peach is a ghastly woman. You can never get a word in edgeways when you meet her and she never listens to you when you can.'

George's remark surprised Marjorie, mainly because it was the first time she had heard George agree with anything Alfreda had to say.

'That's not the point,' she replied. 'The point is that Alfreda seems to take delight in being charming to people's faces and rude about them behind their backs. It's deceitful and hypocritical, and I don't like it. She never used to be like this. She doesn't have a good word to say about anyone. I hardly recognise my little girl any more.'

At that moment, Marjorie's little girl came out of the front door.

'There she is,' said George with a smile. 'Morning Alfreda.'

'Good morning, Father. Wasting your time on pointless activities again I see!' said Alfreda, spotting the empty bucket in George's hand.

'No,' retorted George. 'I was giving the car . . .'

'It will simply rain and then you'll just have to wash it all over again. It is extraordinary how some people will fritter away their time on such foolishness. Mother, I am going to visit young Parkway. I shall be back in time for luncheon.'

Marjorie shrugged her shoulders as Alfreda walked off down the road towards Parkway's house.

'She's still got that cold, Marjorie,' said George in a concerned tone.

In the event, Alfreda found herself back at home long before luncheon. She had turned up at Parkway's and he answered the door to her. He stood in the doorway.

'Hello, Alf.'

'Good morning, dear boy. I trust you are well, that I find you in good spirits?'

'Yeah. All right,' he said, not very convincingly.

There was a moment's pause before Alfreda asked:

'Well, are you going to stand there like some officious hotel doorman waiting for a tip, or are you going to invite me in?'

'It's just that I've got a lot of jobs to do for my mum.'

'In that case, my young friend, I can be of some assistance perhaps.'

'No, it's all right,' he replied hastily. 'They're all dead boring.'

Alfreda stood looking at Parkway, who was looking at his feet. Eventually she asked:

'Have I done something to upset you?'

'No,' Parkway replied. 'It's just . . . .'

'Yes.'

'It's just . . . . it's just you don't ask me any riddles any more, or write any silly poems, or tell me any jokes.'

'Oh!' said Alfreda, genuinely surprised. 'Is that all! Very well. Now . . . . let's see . . . a joke . . . . yes.'

Alfreda had to think for quite some time before she came up with the following:

'Why does one need holes in one's trousers?'

'To put your legs through,' answered Parkway, glumly.

'Ah, so you have heard that one before. Never mind. There are plenty more where that came from, don't you know!'

But as Alfreda tried remembering another joke, nothing sprang to mind. She searched and searched, but even among the deepest recesses of her memory, none was to be found. It was as if the stream had dried up and no amount of dredging was going to bring another one to the surface. In the end she had to admit defeat, and in a profoundly serious voice, she said:

'This is all very well, Master Parkway, but, you know, jokes are such Paltry Things. Grrreat Poetry, on the other hand . . .! Jokes may come and go, but Great Poetry is immortal!'

Parkway continued to stare at his feet.

'Yeah, well, anyway, I'd better go and do these jobs for my mum. See you, Alf.'

And with that, Parkway reluctantly closed the door.

Alfreda got a similar sort of reaction from April and Sheila. Whereas Parkway found Alfreda embarrassing, especially when she called him 'dear boy', April and Sheila found her either boring or very vain and pompous. So as the summer holidays wore on, Alfreda spent more and more time on her own, mostly in the park opposite the Abbots' house. Here she would wander around addressing the trees in deep, velvety tones:

'Oh Great and Noble tree, Majestic and Alone. You have no concern for frail human affairs!'

It was on one such occasion, as she was in the middle of reciting a Poem in Praise of a Woodlouse, that she noticed three figures coming in her direction. Three figures she had no wish to meet. She ducked behind a great and noble tree, and peeked round the left side to see two of the figures approaching. Turning to her right, she walked straight into— Eddie Jennings.

'Hello, Abbot,' he said with a menacing smile.

'Ah, Master Jennings!' Alfreda replied nervously, surrounded by the three. 'Taking some air? Out for an afternoon stroll?'

'You could say that.'

'Excellent. I myself am enjoying the Delights of Nature in this place. Listen. There. The sweet song of the Cuckoo.'

'It's a pigeon,' Eddie said without smiling.

'Huh! I find it surprising that a Clod like you can tell the difference!' Alfreda said pompously, then wished she hadn't.

'Your trouble is you just don't learn, Abbot, and we're here to teach you a bit of a lesson. I did warn you, but you're a bit slow on the uptake, aren't you?'

'And you, sir, are a Rogue and a damned Scoundrel. I loathe and despise you. I fear not your threats and menaces!'

'What's she talking about?' asked one of Eddie's friends.

'I dunno,' replied Eddie, 'but I reckon the only way to deal with her is to give her a fat lip.'

As Eddie raised a clenched fist, Alfreda put her arms over her head to defend herself and cried out in a blaring voice:

'Help! Murder! Murder! Oh that I should be struck down at such a tender age, in my prime by this band of brigands! oh tragical life! oh cruel, cruel fate!'

Several people in the park stopped and looked round to see where this roaring and trumpeting was coming from. The three brigands stood there not knowing what to do.

'You're not really going to murder her, are you, Eddie?'

'Don't be stupid. Just frighten her a bit, that's all.'

However, it had become clear to Alfreda that the band of brigands was more frightened than she was. She removed her hands from her head, stared at each of them through narrowed eyes and said:

'Back! Back, I say! and learn to respect that which you have dared to trifle with! A woman's honour!'

'Oi, you boys! Leave that little girl alone!'

A park keeper, waving a stick, came running up. Eddie Jennings just had time to call Alfreda 'a nutter' before the three of them ran off.

'Are you all right, love?' asked the keeper. 'Those nasty boys didn't hurt you, did they?'

'I am perfectly well, thank you, my man. I was merely rehearsing some lines from a play I am due to appear in. Rather a fine performance, didn't you think!'

Alfreda was looking pleased with herself. She gave a stiff bow and left the park keeper scratching his head in bewilderment.

Chapter 12

There was one place to which Norbert Quire's fame had not yet spread. This was a small village called Little Dimming, which was where Norbert's Aunt Cecily lived.

Little Dimming lay at the head of a valley where two lines of gently sloping, wooded hills met. It was a peaceful, unhurried community. The pace of life there took its lead from the snail and little ever changed. You could be confident that the years would follow the same pattern and that nothing would be allowed to upset that pattern. Take Mr Trott, for example.

Mr Trott ran the village post office and he knew that each year, at the beginning of June, somebody would call round at his house and ask him to donate something for the provisions stall at the village fête. When this happened, he would go to the cupboard in his kitchen and take out a jar of jam and a tin of tuna. This was his donation. On the day of the fête he would go up to the provisions stall and buy the jar of jam and tin of tuna, take them home and put them in his cupboard. This way he'd have something to donate to the provisions stall next year. He'd been doing this for the past twenty three years. The jam had long since gone mouldy and the tin of tuna had begun to rust. So there was little danger that anybody other than Mr Trott would buy them from the stall.

This is not to say that changes *never* occurred in Little Dimming. Some years ago, the weathercock on top of the church tower was repainted, transformed from a dull, scraggy-looking chicken into a splendid, brightly coloured cockerel. However, it was only many years later that anybody noticed. Frank Gurney was sitting in the pub and he made the following announcement to anybody who happened to be listening:

'I see they gone and painted the weathercock.'

The pub fell silent. Everybody turned and looked at Frank in disbelief.

'Don't be daft,' said Trevor behind the bar, ' 'course they haven't.' Old Bob in the corner added:

'I've lived in this village for nigh on sixty-five year and I never seen the weathercock painted.'

'Well go and 'ave a look then if you don't believe me!' said Frank indignantly.

The inmates of the pub piled out of the door and stood in the car-park staring up at the church tower across the road. By now, the winds and rain of many winters had tarnished the gold of his body and flaked the red paint off his comb. The weathercock was reduced to his former wretched state.

'What did I tell you!' said Trevor, smugly. ' 'E's bin like that since I were a lad.'

'That's going back a bit then, Trev.'

'You watch your mouth, young Barry,' he replied as he went back inside the pub. The others followed on behind, muttering about Frank:

'Silly old fool!'

'Too much cider, that's the trouble.'

Frank stayed a little longer looking up at the weathercock

before he too returned inside, all the time wondering how he'd ever got to thinking that it had been repainted.

Norbert was Aunt Cecily's favourite nephew and she had always been his most ardent fan. As she hadn't seen or heard from him for some time, she wrote and invited him to come and have tea with her. Norbert was delighted. Not only was he fond of Aunt Cecily, but he loved being in the country. The only problem was when he could get away, what with all the recitals and performances Monty Banks had arranged for him. However, he found a free day and wrote to Aunt Cecily to tell her when he'd be coming.

On the day she received her nephew's note, Aunt Cecily bumped into Mrs Pickles, the vicar's wife, and Mrs Smallwood, outside the village shop. She waved the note at them.

'From my nephew, Norbert Quire,' she said proudly.

'The actor?' asked Mrs Pickles.

'That's the one,' Cecily replied. 'He's coming for tea.' Then an idea struck Cecily. 'In fact, the two of you must come round to tea as well, to meet him. Next Tuesday.'

'I feel I know him well already, you've told us so much about him, Cecily,' said Mrs Smallwood.

'We'd love to come, Cecily. Have you seen your nephew on stage lately?' asked the vicar's wife.

'Not lately. The last time I saw him he was playing the Hunchback of Notre Dame. Though I say it myself, he was brilliant. That voice of his! One moment it would sound so terrifying and violent, the next so sad and moving it almost brought tears to my eyes. With a bit of luck he'll give us a little performance after tea.'

'We'll look forward to it,' said Mrs Smallwood.

'Tuesday, then. Oh, and don't forget to ask the Major, Daphne. He'd be most welcome too.'

The Major was Daphne Smallwood's husband. A retired army officer, he was well known around Little Dimming for his attempts at training ferrets to carry coded messages to a friend of his in a nearby village.

The following Tuesday, Norbert arrived at the railway station

88

and poked his head in at the ticket office window. The booking clerk had his back to the window. He was sorting a pile of tickets.

'Er, Little Dimwit, please,' asked Norbert.

'Where was that, miss? . . . . ooh! Sorry, sir!' said the clerk as he turned round to see Norbert's grinning face at the glass.

'Where did you say you wanted to go?'

'Little Dimming.'

'Single?' asked the clerk.

'No, divorced,' Norbert piped.

The clerk sighed.

'Will you be returning from Little Dimming, sir?'

'Yeah, 'fraid so,' said Norbert.

Mr Quire paid for his ticket and wandered off down the other end of the platform. The booking clerk watched him go and said:

'So am I, sir.'

Norbert sat down on a hard, wooden bench and waited for the train to appear. When it did, he stepped into a carriage which already contained three other passengers. He sat by the window, said ' 'ello' to the man sitting next to him and watched the station slide past as the train pulled out. The man sitting next to Norbert seemed a little nervous. He pulled out a newspaper and hid behind it. Norbert tapped him on the hand:

'I promise I won't read your newspaper on this side,' he said.

The man ignored this remark and Norbert sat in the corner with his arms folded. After a while, rocked by the gentle rhythm of the train and the sound of the wheels calling out 'Little Dimming little dimming little dimming little dimming' as they trundled along, Norbert fell asleep.

He awoke as the train pulled into the station. He got out of the carriage and set off to walk the two miles or so, down the green, sun-filled lanes, to Aunt Cecily's house.

When Norbert rang the door bell he was greeted by Aunt Cecily still wearing her oven gloves. He leant down to give her a kiss on the cheek.

' 'ello, Aunt Celery,' he said.

She stepped back for a moment and stared closely at the

figure standing in front of her. It certainly *looked* like Norbert, but . . . .

'Norbert??!! That is you, isn't it?' she asked.

' 'course it's me, Aunty! Who d'you think it is? Queen Boodiwhatsit?'

'It's lovely to see you, dear. Do come in. You're a little bit early. The others haven't arrived yet. Go in and sit down. I'll be with you in a minute.'

Norbert went into the drawing room, blew a raspberry at Cecily's cat and sat down. When the other guests arrived, Norbert was introduced to each of them in turn by his Aunt.

'This is Mrs Pickles, the vicar's wife.'

'Mrs Vickers, the pickle's wife,' Norbert repeated.

'Pleased to meet you, Mr Quire. Cecily has told us a great deal about you.'

Then Cecily introduced Norbert to Major and Mrs Small-wood. For one moment, she thought that Norbert had referred to them as Major and Mrs Smallhead, but she must have misheard him. She then returned to the kitchen to finish her preparations for tea, leaving her guests sitting in an uneasy silence which was broken by Mrs Pickles asking:

'It must be very interesting to be an actor, Mr Quire?'

'It's all right,' he replied with a shrug of his shoulders.

The silence returned. Then Daphne Smallwood said:

'Cecily is a very generous woman, don't you think? You're lucky to have such a nice person for an aunt!'

'Aunt Celery? Yeah, she's a good old stick.' Norbert spluttered with laughter at this joke, but when he saw the unsmiling faces of the other three guests, he stopped, sighed, and glanced around the room.

'You interested in ferrets, Mr Quire?' asked the Major at length.

'Geoffrey!!!' interrupted his wife. 'I don't think a distinguished actor like Mr Quire would be interested in such things!'

'I saw a bloke on telly once stick one down his trousers,' Norbert said.

'Oooh!' said Daphne, delicately. 'That sounds rather cruel.'

'Very intelligent creatures, ferrets,' continued the Major,

now he'd got onto his favourite topic of conversation.

'They can swim well,' Norbert added.

'Really, I didn't know that. I am surprised.'

'I heard of this ferret that swam to France,' Norbert went on.

'Extraordinary. They really are the most astonishing creatures.'

'It was a cross-channel ferret.' Norbert hooted with laughter. He was getting into his stride and beginning to enjoy himself. He decided to ask a few riddles.

Over the next twenty minutes or so, as Aunt Cecily busied herself in the kitchen pulling cakes out of the oven, cutting cucumber and making tea, she heard, coming from the other room every now and again, these high-pitched peals of laughter. She was rather confused by this. It couldn't be the Major, and it certainly wasn't Norbert. As far as she knew, Norbert didn't even know how to laugh. It didn't sound like Mrs Pickles, which only left Daphne. But Daphne was quite a severe woman. Cecily couldn't imagine her giggling in that school-girl fashion. Unless, of course . . . . but no. She was very surprised, then, when she pushed the laden trolley in through the door of the drawing room, to find Norbert standing up in the middle of the room, swinging his arms around and asking Mrs Pickles what you get if you cross a duck with a wellington boot. Only a mouthful of sandwich and a cup of tea brought an end to Norbert's riddles.

Cecily was beginning to worry about her nephew. He was behaving most strangely. Perhaps he'd been working too hard and the strain was getting to him. The other guests were not so much worried as bewildered by Mr Quire. Cecily had told them over and over again how serious and impressive her nephew was, how his deep voice had sometimes made the china ornaments on her mantelpiece rattle when he spoke. This was not the Mr Quire they had been led to expect.

Norbert restored his reputation a little during tea, simply by saying nothing. In fact he was bored by the conversation about village matters and found it more interesting to stare into his tea-cup and wonder what it was like to be a tea leaf.

After tea, Aunt Cecily asked her nephew if he wouldn't mind reciting a little something for the entertainment of herself and her friends, a speech from his latest play perhaps, something dramatic, or tender even?

'I've got a poem, Aunty. I made it up myself.'

'Oh, wonderful!' Cecily said, clasping her hands together.

Norbert stood up in the middle of the room and three pairs of eyes fixed themselves on him. The fourth pair were slowly disappearing under their eyelids as the Major, slumped in an armchair, drifted off to sleep.

'My latest poem,' announced Norbert. 'Called "My Bottom talks to Strangers".'

Mrs Pickles and Mrs Smallwood shifted uneasily in their seats, and Aunt Cecily smiled nervously. All the time she was praying that she hadn't heard what she thought she'd heard. Norbert began:

> My bottom talks to strangers.
> It talks behind my back.
> It sometimes only whispers,
> But I can hear it black-
> ening my name.
>
> People usually pass it by,
> Ignore it, aren't amused.
> But some will say: 'The cheek of it!'
> And think they've been abused,
> or worse.
>
> For those who stop and listen,
> It tells tales about my past.
> It knows I get embarrassed,
> But that just makes the tales last
> even longer.
>
> I just can't shut it up. You see,
> The predicament I'm in.
> Once it starts to blabber,
> All I can do is grin,
> And bear it.

It's not difficult to imagine the reaction of the three good ladies of Little Dimming. They looked like they'd been turned to stone. Horror and disbelief were frozen on their faces. Their mouths gaped open, their eyes were wide, staring at the poet without blinking. Norbert assumed that this was because they were bowled over by his poem, which, in a way, was true. He was on the point of suggesting another poem when the Major in his armchair gave a loud snort and woke himself up. Realising that Norbert had come to the end of his poem, he began applauding.

'Jolly good, young fellah. First rate.'

The snort and the applause also seemed to snap the three ladies out of their trance. Daphne scowled at her husband who stopped clapping immediately. Mrs Pickles seemed to be waking from a nightmare. She got to her feet and made a hasty apology:

'I'm afraid I must be going. The vicar will be expecting his dinner.'

'I got some more poems,' said Norbert, eagerly.

'Thank you, Mr Quire, but I really must be off. Listening to you was sheer . . . I can't remember when I've been quite so . . . er . . . I hope we'll meet again soon.'

Mrs Smallwood also decided that it was time they left.

'Come along, Geoffrey,' she snapped, and the Major heaved himself out of his chair and followed her, inviting Norbert to visit his ferrets whenever he wanted to.

Norbert waited while Aunt Cecily saw her guests out, and when she returned he noticed a look on her face he'd never seen before. It was as if a dark storm cloud had crossed her face and the storm was just about to break. Norbert hunched his shoulders, expecting the thunder and lightning to crash and spark about his ears at any moment. He hoped a cheery remark might calm the storm a little:

'They enjoyed the poem,' he said, tentatively.

The storm broke.

'**What? Enjoyed it?** Don't be a fool, Norbert. They were **horrified**.' Aunt Cecily paused for a moment to compose herself.

'And so was I. I'm just thankful the Major fell asleep and didn't hear that childish, dirty little poem you came out with. They came here expecting something deeply moving and you end up reciting this silly poem about . . . . about . . . . I can't even bring myself to say it. How could you do it, Norbert?'

Norbert Quire was devastated. Aunt Cecily had never been angry with him before, and now he was desperate to explain, to explain that he just wanted to make them all laugh, because there was nothing better than laughing. But the harder he tried the more difficult it became. He couldn't find the words he wanted to explain what he meant. It was as if his voice didn't contain the words he needed to make Aunt Cecily understand. He ummed and ahhed and shifted from foot to foot, increasingly frustrated that he couldn't find the right expression. In the end all he could manage was:

'Sorry, Aunt Celery. Didn't mean to.'

'I think it would be best if you left, Norbert,' she replied.

Norbert fetched his hat and coat, and at the front door he asked:

'Want a hand with the washing up?'

'No. Thank you.'

'Sorry, Aunt Celery.'

'Stop calling me that silly name and talking in that silly voice.'

'Can't help it,' said Norbert as the door closed behind him.

On the long walk back to the station, Norbert got to thinking that he'd have to be a bit more careful in future. This voice was all very well, but sometimes it went too far and carried him away with it. He felt genuinely sorry about what had happened at Aunt Cecily's and would do all he could to make it up to her. In the meantime, tomorrow was another day, and another performance. And with that thought his step lightened.

Chapter 13

The only one who spent any time in Alfreda's company now was Reg. It didn't worry him that she spoke in this strange way. In fact he found her more interesting. This was due mainly to Alfreda's new-found passion for acting. Reg had always wanted to be an actor. Some of his family had been on the stage and even appeared on television. He felt sure the theatre was in his blood. To begin with, it was Alfreda who decided which plays they would perform. She would also play the leading role and be the director. Reg, on the other hand, would be allowed to move any scenery around, clap and cheer at the end of Alfreda's performance, and play any dead characters. He was particularly good at playing dead. All those hours spent sleeping had kept him in practice for these roles. Clapping he was less good at. He produced not so much a 'clap' as a dull 'thud' from his paws.

However, after a while, Reg got fed up with playing second fiddle to Alfreda. She got all the best lines, she strutted around the sitting room declaiming in a deep, sonorous voice, wrapped in a cloak, glowering at a non-existent audience.

'Why can't I be the hero for a change?' Reg asked in a disgruntled manner.

'Don't be so foolish, Reginald. *I* am the one who plays the hero. This role requires an actor of my great talent. It was *not* written for a dog!'

'Well why can't we do a play that has a dog as the hero?'

'Because there *is* none,' Alfreda replied curtly.

'In that case we could make one up.' Reg got quite excited at this idea. 'We could call it *Reg's Day*.'

'A play based on what happens to *you* in an average day would be exceedingly dull.'

'No, I don't mean that,' said Reg. 'I mean a play about what happened to me on the day I had my day.'

'What the dickens are you talking about, Reginald? I sometimes think you have quite taken leave of your senses.'

Reg realised that he was going to have to spell it all out for Alfreda.

'You know that every dog has their day, right? Well, I had my day not very long ago.' Reg hesitated, obviously turning something over in his mind. Then he said:

'I could tell you about it.'

'Oh very well,' Alfreda replied in a bored tone of voice.

Reg looked around him to make sure there wasn't anybody else in the room, and dropping his voice to a whisper, he said:

'It began like this. I was stopped in the street one day by an old blind man, who knew me although he couldn't see me. And he told . .'

'I don't think it's wise talking to members of the public like that,' Alfreda interrupted.

'Yes, well, he told me when my Day was, and that I had to be at the railway station at . . .'

'I don't like railway stations myself. I find them filthy, noisy and crowded with *all* manner of undesirable persons.'

Reg ignored this interruption.

'I was a bit wary of this blind man at first. It could have been a hoax. That's why we don't like talking about it, in case unscrupulous humans try and take advantage of us. But the blind man's dog gave me the wink and I knew . . .'

'I find winking a very vulgar habit, especially in public,' Alfreda interrupted.

'Right. That's it,' Reg said quietly. 'No more. I offer to tell you my story, and all you do is interrupt. You're not listening, are you? So why should I bother! No more story, no more plays, and no more applause!'

Alfreda was positively shocked as she watched Reg walk away. It was only then as she stood alone in the empty room that she realised how far things had gone. This voice, which had made her sound so clever, so full of authority and confidence had bored, bullied or frightened her friends so that now, even Reg, Reg who would have stuck with her through thick and thin, even he'd had enough and wanted no more to do with her. He was right. It was a voice that never listened to anything but itself, a voice without a laugh, such a serious voice, and self-important, full of impressive, but empty, noises. In that moment Alfreda decided that she too had had enough of it. She ran after her dog and found him sitting in his basket. She threw her arms round his neck and in a voice verging on manly tears, she said:

'Not you too, Reginald. Oh do not desert me in my hour of need. I want my old voice back. My poor, lost voice! Lost, gone, kidnapped even! Out there somewhere! You must assist me. You must help me find it.'

Reg would have liked to say something in reply, something along the lines of 'Get off!' or 'Stop being so dramatic!', but he was being held so firmly round the neck by Alfreda that he could barely breathe, let alone say anything. It was probably just as well, because in fact there wasn't much *he* could do. However, he did know someone who he thought might be able to help.

Blah...Blah...Blah...

A BORING OLD BOOK BY A BORING AUTHOR

YAWN

Chapter 14

It had always annoyed Alfreda, for no good reason, that Reg had friends she knew nothing about. So she was not in a particularly good mood as she followed him down a tree-lined avenue to the house where Joyce Vox lived.

In fact, Reg had not known Mrs Vox very long. They had met one morning when Reg, lying under a bush in the front garden, was staking out a multi-million dollar drugs deal taking place between Marjorie and the milkman. His attention was suddenly diverted by the sound of a whistle which was so piercing that only he and any other dog around could have heard it. After a while it began to hurt his ears and he stuck his head out of the bush to find out where it was coming from. It was then he spotted this curious old woman walking along with her hands behind her back looking down at her feet.

'Get out of that bush, Reg!' Marjorie shouted when she saw him.

Reg crawled out just as the curious old woman walked past.

'You realise you've blown my cover!' Reg snarled at her. 'If I don't find Mr Big, it'll be your fault.'

The woman stopped and looked down at Reg.

'Good Lord! A talking dog!' she said. 'I haven't come across one of those for years. What's your name?'

'RRRRRRRReg,' he answered, irritated.

'Pleased to meet you, Reg. I'm Mrs Vox. Joyce Vox. Yes. A talking dog. Goodness me! You don't by any chance know an Irish setter called O'Driscoll, do you?'

All at once, Reg's mood brightened considerably.

'Yes. In fact, he's a cousin of mine.'

'Well I never!' said Mrs Vox. 'I listened to him sing once and I thought he had the finest tenor voice of any dog I'd heard, then or since.' Mrs Vox paused and then added, hesitantly: 'Of course, there aren't many of you left now, are there?'

'No, not many,' Reg replied in a tone that was both proud and sad.

'Still, I'm glad I bumped into you. I've got a recording of O'Driscoll if you want to come and listen to it sometime. Also, I'd very much like to tape you.'

Reg grinned, said he'd be pleased to visit her, and Mrs Vox left her address with him. It was this address that Reg and Alfreda were trying to find somewhere down this tree-lined avenue.

'Where on *earth* are you taking me?' asked Alfreda.

'You said you wanted my help. Well, I think this woman might do the trick,' Reg replied.

The two of them counted the numbers of the well-kept houses until they reached the one where Mrs Vox should have lived. At first they almost missed the house, hidden as it was by a high hedge. Behind the hedge grew a tangled profusion of weeds, brambles and tall trees. These shut out much of the light, making the house look dark and forbidding. Reg and Alfreda walked up the path to the front door, brushing aside twigs and branches as they went. Alfreda was just looking for the doorbell, when the door opened and Mrs Vox appeared.

'Ah, Reg. I thought I heard you coming up the path. Do come in.'

Reg and Alfreda stepped into a dimly-lit hallway. In front of them, a staircase rose into the darkness of the upstairs. Alfreda ran her hand over the faded brown wallpaper and became aware of the almost total quiet of the house.

'This is my friend, Alfreda Abbot,' said Reg.

Alfreda turned towards the elderly woman with short white hair dressed in a green skirt and a purple cardigan.

'How do you do, Madam,' said Alfreda.

'Very well, thank you,' she replied, and looked at Alfreda for a moment, which made Alfreda feel uneasy.

'Mmmm, interesting!' Mrs Vox said finally. 'Your friend, Reg, has got somebody else's voice.'

'Blimey, that was quick work!' Reg said. 'I told you she could help.'

Alfreda was less enthusiastic.

'I am well aware of the problem, Madam. The question is, can you provide the solution?'

'We can try,' replied Joyce Vox. 'There's nothing very unusual about this. People are forever fiddling around with others' voices, making them say things they don't want to say, stopping them from talking the way they want to talk, or simply telling them to shut up. They take the words out of one person's mouth and put words into another person's mouth. It's all very unhygienic, if you ask me, and the sooner it stops the better. Anyway, no point standing in the hallway!'

Mrs Vox opened the door to the left and Reg and Alfreda followed her into the front room. This was even gloomier than the hallway. The half-closed curtains on the windows blocked out what little light had managed to get through the thick growth of bushes and trees outside. Alfreda's eyes were just getting used to the gloom when Mrs Vox turned on a small lamp, the glow from which lit up what could only be described as 'a shambles'. The walls of the room were lined with shelves, each one of which was packed with enormous books, huge leather-bound volumes. Many of them were falling apart or covered in dust. The tables and chairs were piled high with books and papers, written in strange, unknown languages. The floor was a spider's web of criss-crossing black wires which led to an array of machines against the far wall; tape-recorders, cassette recorders, amplifiers, banks of speakers, phonographs, radiograms, oscilloscopes, stethoscopes, headphones, otoscopes, an audiophone, gramophones and a megaphone.

Alfreda sat down in the middle of the spider's web because all the chairs were taken up with books and papers or equipment. Reg sat next to her and she put her arm around him, which made them both feel better. She cast her eyes around the room. She'd never seen anything like it and was curious to know more about the equipment that lay around.

'What is the purpose of these contraptions?' she asked.

Mrs Vox thought for a moment and answered:

'Cages.'

Reg gulped rather louder than he had meant to. It was a reply which made neither him nor Alfreda feel any more comfortable. In fact he was beginning to wonder if he hadn't been a bit hasty in suggesting that Mrs Vox would be the one to help Alfreda.

'Cages?' asked Alfreda, not understanding what Mrs Vox meant.

'Sort of. Some people capture animals and keep them in cages to study them. I capture sounds.'

'Sounds?' Alfreda repeated, still not understanding.

'Are you repeating everything I say, or is there an echo in here?' asked Mrs Vox with a grin.

'Well you're *not* making yourself very clear, woman,' Alfreda snapped.

'Mmmmm!' said Mrs Vox, 'the sooner you get your old voice back the better. I'm not sure I like the one you've got very much. Right, let me explain. What interests me are those sounds which are rarely heard or often ignored. In fact, some people don't even know they exist. Listen to this, for example.'

Mrs Vox went over to a tape recorder and wound the tape on until the counter read 694. Then she pressed 'play'.

Alfreda listened . . . .

and heard nothing. But Reg turned his head to one side and a grin lit up his face.

'It's the Twilight Song of the Earthworm,' he said, 'such a sad song and what a wonderful recording!'

'Well done, Reg. Dogs have such sensitive ears!' Mrs Vox ran the tape back until it reached 367 and played it again.

'This is a sound you hear thousands of times a day,' she said.

Alfreda listened . . . .

and heard nothing. Neither did Reg.

'That's the sound of eyelids opening and shutting. It's probably the most common sound you ever hear. What about this one?'

Mrs Vox tried several more, including the sound of an old man remembering and a rare recording of Pigs at Prayer. Although Reg recognised some of them, Alfreda heard nothing.

'Your hearing's not very good, is it, my dear?' said Mrs Vox. 'Or perhaps you don't pay enough attention.'

By now, Alfreda was getting impatient.

'These foolish games are all very well, but how are they going to help get my voice back, my poor, lost voice, out there, somewhere, all alone and friendless, perhaps frightened . . .'

'All right, all right,' said Mrs Vox, 'let's not get over-dramatic about this. First of all I'm going to have to find out whose voice you've got, and you're going to have to give me as many clues as possible. Now, what do we know already? It's probably a man's voice, forty years old maybe. There, that's narrowed the field down to half a million already. What I want *you* to do, Alfreda, is to talk and talk and talk . . .'

'I'm not sure she'll be able to manage that,' said Reg sarcastically.

Alfreda was not amused and she flicked the end of his nose, which always made his eyes water.

'Start by telling me something about yourself,' said Mrs Vox.

'Well . . let's see . . it's now a little over eleven years since my first appearance on the Stage of Life. In that time the parts I have played have been modest, although I have confidence that my talents and destiny will lead me to play one of Life's Grrreat roles, and that . .'

'Good Lord, you sound like a boring old book,' said Joyce. 'Go on.'

And so, in her deep, velvety and resonant tones, Alfreda went on, and on, and on, and on, and on. All the time, Joyce Vox stood quite still in the middle of the room listening, listening intently to what Alfreda was saying. Reg could see the effort she was putting into it. Then she went over to the shelves and scanned the massive volumes until she found the one she was looking for. She hitched up her skirt, stepped up on to a chair and pulled the book from its place. She was surprisingly agile for her age, thought Reg. She sprang down off the chair with the heavy book in her hands and began leafing through the pages, running her finger up and down the columns of countless names printed there.

'Useless,' she said. 'Out of date.' And she let the book fall to the floor with a crash. A luminous green glow then filled the room as Mrs Vox switched on her computer and fed in a disc. She scanned the unending list of names that the machine churned out. Every now and then she'd raise her head and listen more intently to what Alfreda was saying. Sometimes Mrs Vox would ask her to repeat a word or phrase. 'How did you pronounce that word?' she'd ask. Or; 'Say that again slowly.'

Next she consulted a small chart which lay on the table.

'That's no good either,' she said, and threw it over her shoulder narrowly missing Reg. So she pulled a large map out of its cardboard tube and unrolled it on the floor. She made Reg sit on one end to keep it flat. Kneeling on the floor, she pored over this map for some time, occasionally muttering things like: 'Bolton perhaps,' or 'definitely not East Anglia.' And all the while Alfreda was talking and talking and talking. She had run out of things to say about herself, so she began reciting poems and speeches from plays in a loud and dramatic voice. Eventually Mrs Vox got to her feet and returned to her computer. She typed a few commands, made a quick calculation, and announced:

'Now we're really beginning to get somewhere. This voice could only belong to 1 out of 56,852 people. What happened to my chart?'

'Under the table, where you threw it,' said Reg. 'Can I get off this map now?'

'Of course you can.'

Reg lay down on the floor while Mrs Vox scrabbled around under the table looking at her chart again. Then suddenly:

'Ah, there it is!' she said triumphantly.

'She has found my voice!' cried Alfreda. 'Oh Joy of Joys!'

'No, I've found my little screwdriver. It's been missing for weeks.'

Reg tried stuffing his paws in his ears and going to sleep. Listening to Alfreda chattering nineteen to the dozen and watching this madwoman crawling around on her hands and knees was getting on his nerves.

Next, Mrs Vox plugged in the oscilloscope and placed a microphone in front of Alfreda. Now, whenever Alfreda spoke, her voice appeared on the screen of the oscilloscope as a jagged, jerky line, like a row of sharp-peaked mountains.

'Come and have a look at this, Reg,' said Mrs Vox. 'It's an interesting shape, don't you think?'

'Oh yes, very interesting,' he agreed, not knowing what on earth he was meant to be looking at.

Joyce Vox spent the next half hour moving between Alfreda's flickering, zig-zag voice on the oscilloscope and the list of numberless names unfolding on the computer screen. Finally, rubbing her eyes and stretching, she said:

'Well, that's the best I can do. I've got it down to four possible names. It shouldn't be too difficult to find out which one this voice belongs to, Alfreda. I'm going to send you home and I shall let you know when I've got some news.'

'Much obliged,' wheezed Alfreda, whose throat was quite sore from all that talking.

Then Reg gave a small cough as if to remind someone of something.

'Whoops, sorry Reg. I almost forgot. I was going to record you, wasn't I. What are you going to say?'

Mrs Vox pulled out a tape marked 'Talking Dogs' and wound it onto a tape recorder. Reg, meantime, couldn't make up his mind what to say. In fact he was feeling rather sheepish about the whole idea, which is not easy for a dog to do. Finally he decided, so that he wouldn't be outdone by his cousin O'Driscoll, he'd sing a song. It was an old sea song called 'The Salty Dog'.

After two verses of the most tuneless singing she'd ever heard, Mrs Vox switched off the tape recorder.

'Thank you, Reg, that'll do nicely.'

'But there are nineteen more verses!' protested Reg.

'Some other time perhaps. I think Alfreda is exhausted and you really ought to see her home.'

'Indeed I am. That was possibly the longest performance of my career so far. I shall hear from you in due course, no doubt.'

'No doubt,' said Mrs Vox.

As they left down the garden path, Mrs Vox couldn't help but overhear Alfreda say to Reg in a gruff tone:

'I just hope that woman knows what she is doing, that's all I can say!'

'I thought she was brilliant!' said Reg.

'Harrrumph! That remains to be seen.'

'I don't think I'd like the person whose voice you've got, you know,' said Reg.

I couldn't agree more, Reg, Mrs Vox was thinking as she returned to the list of four names on the table. She still had some work to do. She decided it would be best if she simply phoned up the four people on the list and saw if she could work out which one was the most likely candidate.

The first two calls were unsuccessful, but on the third, a high-pitched voice piped out in response:

' 'ello, Norby Quire here.'

Mrs Vox put down the phone without saying anything. So, Norbert Quire the performing poet had Alfreda's voice. Mrs Vox remembered hearing him on the radio reciting some of his stories and poems, and she was astonished at the time by how convincing he sounded. For a long time, Mrs Vox had wanted to meet Mr Quire. Now she had the opportunity.

Chapter 15

Before getting in contact with Mr Quire, something made Joyce Vox decide to find out some more about him. She tracked down one of Norbert's old friends, an actor like himself. From him, Joyce Vox learned about the curious change that had come over Mr Norbert Quire, how he'd been transformed from this deadly serious, pompous, tragic actor with a booming resonant voice, into a madcap poet and story-teller with the voice of a young girl. This got Mrs Vox thinking. If Norbert's success was due to Alfreda's voice, the last thing he'd want to do would be to give it up and accept his old voice in return. That being the case, Mrs Vox was going to have to be rather more cunning, if Alfreda's voice was to be returned to her. She set about devising a plan.

A week or so later, Norbert was coming out of the stage door of a large theatre with Monty Banks. Monty had his arm around Norbert's shoulder and was poking him jovially in the chest:

'Well done, old son. Another sell-out. Keep up the good work. I'm negotiating a little deal which will really put you on the map. I'll tell you more about it when I've got some news. Now, don't forget, you're at the Theatre Royal on Friday. I'll come and pick you up, all right?'

'Yeah.' Norbert replied. 'And Monty? Can I have some more pocket money?'

'Already! I only gave you some the other day!'

'Oh go on! Pleeeease.'

'I don't know what you do with it all,' Monty said, peeling a couple of five pound notes from a fat roll he kept in his pocket.

'Ta. See you next week.' And Norbert went off towards the bus station.

At that moment, Mrs Vox stepped out of the shadows carrying a large battered suitcase, and hurried after him. She caught up with him and introduced herself as the two of them walked in step.

'I'd like to say how much I enjoyed your performance tonight, Mr Quire.'

'Thanks,' said Norbert with a grin.

'I particularly liked the story of the man who thought he'd been turned into a bird by the one-eyed carpet seller.'

'Yeah. That's dead good, that one. I like the bit when the old man falls out of bed and lands on top of the robber who thinks it really *is* a flying pig.'

Norbert and Mrs Vox both started laughing together.

'And then,' said Norbert, catching his breath between laughs, 'and then, he beats up the old woman thinking it's his brother dressed up as his wife in disguise.'

By now, Norbert was almost helpless with laughter and had to lean against a wall to stop himself falling over. He and Mrs Vox strolled on towards the bus station, recalling tales and poems from the evening performance, and then sat in the brightly lit bus station café while Norbert asked her every riddle he had heard. Astonishingly, she knew the answer to every single one, which impressed Norbert no end. After twenty minutes and five banana milk shakes, Norbert said he had to catch his bus. Mrs Vox said she had greatly enjoyed talking with him, that she would be at his next performance, and it was a pity about his problem.

'Eh? What? What problem?' asked Norbert, suddenly confused.

'Oh, it's nothing. It's not important,' said Mrs Vox. 'You'd better hurry or you'll miss your bus.'

'No! Come on! Don't be like that! Tell me!' Norbert was hopping around wondering whether to catch his bus or find out what this problem might be.

'All right. Look, I can go in your direction. I'll catch the same bus.'

Mrs Vox picked up the battered suitcase and followed Norbert at top speed across the tarmac of the bus station. Once on board, Norbert asked again about this 'problem'.

'Best not to talk about it in public,' whispered Mrs Vox.

Norbert agreed, then he asked:

'Has your case got a name, Mrs Fox?'

'No, Mr Quire, it hasn't.'

'It ought to have one.'

'Why?'

'Justin Case.' Norbert snorted with laughter so loudly that the couple sitting in front of him turned round and gave him a very odd look.

Mrs Vox turned the other way, as if this man was nothing to do with her.

By the time the bus reached his stop, Norbert was so desperate to find out what Mrs Vox was talking about he asked her to come up to his flat and tell him about it. He offered to carry her case up the stairs, but when he tried to lift it he found it was so heavy he could hardly raise it off the floor.

'Blimey, what've you got in here? A sack of potatoes?'

'The tools of my trade,' replied Mrs Vox.

'You're not a blacksmith, are you?'

In the drawing room of Norbert's flat, Mrs Vox began to explain how she had been sitting at the back of the theatre during Norbert's performance and often it was difficult to hear what he was saying.

'This was a great disappointment to me, one of your biggest fans,' she said. 'The problem is that as more and more people come to hear you, you'll have to perform in bigger and bigger places. Now, imagine what would happen if thousands of your fans packed into a hall and only a handful could hear you? There'd be a riot! People would start demanding their money back!'

Norbert was deeply worried by this prospect.

'Monty wouldn't like that. And I'd get the blame for it, I expect, as usual.'

'Exactly,' said Joyce Vox. 'And the solution to this problem is . . . . a bigger voice, one large enough to *fill* a concert hall, or a football stadium.'

'Hang on a minute,' Norbert objected. 'Why can't I just use a microphone?'

Mrs Vox looked horrified.

'A microphone! A microphone! Mr Quire, as one of your most ardent admirers, I must protest. If we, your adoring fans, have to listen to you through a microphone, distorting the wonderful music of your voice, it wouldn't be worth coming to hear you at all! We might just as well stay at home and listen to a bad recording on a cheap record player!'

Now Norbert felt awkward and was sorry he had mentioned the microphone at all. Mrs Vox continued:

'I think my solution is best. And, after all, why stop at a football stadium . . . Imagine, Mr Quire . . . Imagine yourself standing on the highest peak of the Black Mountains of Wales, holding a book of your poems, and a voice so vast that when you start talking, miles away the population of Birmingham would stand quite still and listen . . . .'

Norbert's eyes took on a far-away stare and Mrs Vox continued her vision in hushed tones:

'. . . people in their houses would turn down their televisions, shoppers would stop in the street, supermarkets would be filled with a deathly hush, motorists would switch off their engines, just to listen, as your voice came ringing in over the city. And then . . . . peals and roars of laughter! A whole city reduced to helpless laughter, people doubled up, or clutching at their sides, tears streaming down their faces! What do you think of that?'

'Yeah,' breathed Norbert, entranced. 'Sounds great! Can you really do that?'

'Of course. Voices are my profession. I've done it for lots of people. The only thing to decide is which size of voice would be best for you.'

Mrs Vox lifted her case on to the table and began removing the contents. She took out glass tubes, flasks, a bunsen burner, wooden cigar boxes, an ear trumpet, string, rubber bands, rather old ham sandwiches, matches, maps, a calculator, compasses, cotton wool, gauze, vials, files, a stethoscope, plastic bags, pens and pencils, tape, chewing gum, a tin of alphabetti spaghetti and a Dancing Master's violin. At the bottom she found what she was looking for—a large, colour brochure. She handed the brochure to Norbert, telling him to look through it and choose the voice he wanted, while she put together her apparatus.

Norbert began leafing through the pages of the brochure. It contained the stories of all those who had called upon Joyce Vox to help them. Here was the opera singer who used to be stuck at the back of the chorus where her voice was drowned out by the others around her. Now, after Mrs Vox's help, she had only starring roles and had to be careful not to shatter all the glass chandeliers in the opera houses. Here too was the little corporal who dreamed of being a Sergeant Major, but could barely be heard even through a megaphone. Now, when he gives the command FFIIIIIIIIIIIIIRRRRRRRRE! at a 21–gun salute, nobody can hear the cannons going off. Norbert was getting more and more excited as he read through the brochure. He found out about the woman who'd earned her living for twenty years as the foghorn on an ocean liner. Her bellow could be heard for thirty-five miles out at sea on a foggy day. Then there was the quarryman who could bring down an avalanche of rock just by shouting into a crack. Or the lumberjack who could fell a giant fir tree with a sneeze. Each voice seemed more powerful and impressive than the last.

However, it was when he reached the last page that Norbert could barely contain himself. His eyes opened wide and he whistled through his teeth. On that last page was the biggest voice of all, a voice that could fill the Universe, a voice that could be heard in the deepest nooks and darkest crannies of the Cosmos.

'Blimey!' Norbert breathed. 'Could you make my voice like that?'

Mrs Vox was attaching a glass flask to a clamp, but she didn't need to look at the brochure to find out which voice Norbert was referring to.

'Everybody asks that,' she said with a laugh. 'The answer is "no". In fact, that's just an artist's impression. I doubt whether a voice that size exists anywhere.'

'What's it doing in the book, then?' asked Norbert, who felt he'd somehow been cheated.

'Makes an interesting story,' replied Mrs Vox, connecting the bunsen burner to a small gas bottle. 'It was a very long time ago, I was asked to draw up plans for this voice, and if I'd known how difficult it was going to be I'd never have agreed from the outset. The problems were colossal. Firstly there was the sheer size of it! Nobody had ever even designed a voice that big, let alone built one! It had to be loud enough to fill the whole Universe and, at the same time, not burst everybody's eardrums whenever it was used. You try making a voice that can send a whisper from one end of the Cosmos to the other! It's not easy, I can tell you!'

'I bet not,' Norbert agreed.

'Then there was the trouble over the tone of the thing. I was told that it had to be full of Power and Majesty without sounding like a tyrant, so it would make people do as they were told without scaring the wits out of them. It had to speak every language under the sun, and all those above it too. The whole thing was a nightmare, Mr Quire.'

'And what if a voice like that let out a burp?' Norbert asked none too seriously.

'You may well laugh, but if that had happened, it could have literally wiped out whole solar systems. I worked on that voice for decades, and in the end I was glad to be rid of it.'

'What happened then?' asked Norbert.

'I handed over the plans I'd drawn up, but at the same time I wrote a report saying that the voice was all very well in theory, but the technical problems were too great and too complicated, and I doubted very much whether it would be possible to build even a prototype. However, my advice was ignored and I was told I didn't know what I was talking about. I also tried to find out who would want a voice that big and for what. But again I was told to mind my own business, so I thought "let them get on with it".'

'So you don't know whether the voice was built or not.'

'No. Some people claim they've heard it, but I'm not convinced. If a voice that size had been bouncing around the Heavens, you'd have thought it would have been heard by more than a handful of folk, wouldn't you!'

'S'pose so,' replied Norbert, who was still feeling disappointed. He really liked the idea of sending a nonsense poem or a joke out across the dark expanses of Space. However, he consoled himself with the thought that even if some space creatures *did* hear it, they probably wouldn't understand it and he'd end up having to explain it to them.

In the end, Mrs Vox persuaded Norbert Quire to settle for a voice of more modest size, one which could be heard over a huge area, without losing any clarity or humour. By now she had finished putting together her apparatus. It stood on Norbert's table looking like nothing so much as a fantastic musical instrument. It had an ear trumpet at one end. In the middle was a twisted confusion of glass tubes, vials and flasks, some containing different coloured liquids, some heated. And at the other end was a glass bulb.

'Right then,' said Mrs Vox in a very business-like manner. 'All we have to do is remove your voice so I can work on it. It's very simple. You talk into the ear trumpet at this end and as your voice goes through all these tubes etcetera it becomes condensed and ends up in the glass bulb at this end. The process takes some time, so we might as well get going.'

'What'll I say?' asked Norbert.

'Oh, anything. It doesn't matter what you say.'

Norbert put his head to the ear trumpet and began talking, saying the first thing that came into his head. For a quarter of an hour he babbled and prattled, chattered and drivelled, gassed, gabbed, blatted, waffled and blethered. And soon Mrs Vox could see a thin vapour beginning to appear in the bulb.

'Can I have a rest now?' croaked Norbert as he began to tire.

'No, no!' Mrs Vox replied. 'You must keep going. It could be disastrous if you stopped now.'

Norbert's throat was feeling dry and sore. His voice was beginning to crack, but he carried on nevertheless. He continued to gabble and gibber, patter, prate and twaddle.

And as his voice began to fade so the vapour in the glass bulb thickened and solidified. After another ten minutes of ranting and burbling, Norbert was left mouthing silent sounds and his voice lay like a little white cornflake in the glass bulb.

'There we are!' exclaimed Mrs Vox, picking up Norbert's voice with a pair of tweezers and putting it into a plastic bag. She wrote his name on a label and attached it to the bag.

Joyce Vox packed away her equipment and explained to Mr Quire that she would return the following evening with his new, super-large turbo-powered voice. At once Norbert's brow furrowed and a worried expression clouded his face. He had thought it would all be done immediately, on the spot. He hoped now that he'd done the right thing. Above all he didn't want to get into trouble with Monty Banks. Mrs Vox read all these wordless questions on his face and tried to set his mind at rest.

'Don't worry, Mr Quire. Your voice is in good hands. I'll see it comes to no harm. In fact, here's my address. If you like you can come round tomorrow and pick up the voice yourself.'

The worried expression disappeared from Norbert's face and was replaced by a grin. He showed Mrs Vox out. Then he returned to his drawing room, while his thoughts returned to that peak in the Black Mountains of Wales.

Chapter 16

At lunchtime on the following day, Monty had arranged to meet Norbert at the pub round the corner from his flat. As usual Norbert was late. So Monty sat in front of a pint of beer with Esmerelda at his side. She sat in front of a glass of Babycham and five empty peanuts packets. Monty was in a very excitable mood. He shifted about in his chair, impatient for the arrival of his star.

'Oh stop fidgeting around, Monty,' ordered Esmerelda. 'You're like a dog with fleas. Go and buy me some more peanuts.'

'Sorry, my love. It's just that I can't wait to tell Norbert the news.'

As Monty was collecting his change from the barman, he

overheard somebody saying: 'That's Norbert Quire, isn't it?' He looked round and saw the poet's head poking round the door. Norbert grinned when he recognised his friend and manager.

'There you are, old son,' remarked Monty cheerily. 'Come and join us. Have I got some news for you!'

Norbert sat on a stool across the table from Monty and Esmerelda.

'Hello Norbert,' said Esmerelda in a bored sort of voice.

Norbert grinned and nodded. Monty leaned forward across the table and said:

'You remember the little deal I was fixing up for you?'

Norbert knitted his brow and thought for a minute. Then he nodded when he remembered that Monty had mentioned something about it outside the theatre yesterday.

'Well, it's come off,' Monty continued. 'I've lined you up to appear at . . . .'

(Here he paused for dramatic effect.)

'. . . the Albert Hall.'

Norbert's eyes lit up.

'Not on your own, of course. There'll be others appearing as well, but . . . . the Albert Hall. What d'you think about that then?'

Norbert sat there grinning.

'Well, say something!'

Norbert gave Monty the thumbs up sign, but said nothing. This annoyed Monty a little. After all, he'd put a lot of effort into getting Norbert signed up and didn't think the poet was showing enough enthusiasm for his success.

'What's the matter with you, Norbert? Anybody would think this sort of thing happened to you every day. Aren't you excited?'

Norbert nodded vigorously.

'Well, say something then!'

The poet was beginning to look a little nervous, uneasy, as if he was trying to hide something. Monty couldn't fail to notice this.

'Come on, old son. Out with it. What's the matter? What have you done?'

Norbert pulled out a scrap of paper from his pocket and hurriedly wrote down on it:

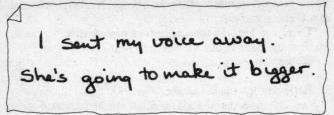

I sent my voice away.
She's going to make it bigger.

Norbert handed the piece of paper to his manager and expected some sort of expression of delight from him. Instead, Monty leapt to his feet nearly knocking a packet of peanuts out of Esmerelda's hand.

'Oi, watch it!' she said. Monty ignored her.

'Have you gone off your trolley? Do you realise what you've done? That voice is my . . our fortune. How could you just let it go like that? Who's got it? Where is it?'

Norbert's face fell, and in a panic of fumbling he began searching through his pockets for the piece of paper with Joyce Vox's name and address on it. Monty sat down and put his head in his hands.

'Don't get so upset, Monty. It's not good for you. Calm down.' Esmerelda tried to soothe her ruffled husband.

'Don't get upset?' he retorted. 'What do you expect me to do? I've just signed him up for the Albert Hall and he goes and gives his voice away to a total stranger! And you tell me not to get upset!'

At this point Norbert handed over the piece of paper Mrs Vox had given him. Monty studied the name and address and shook his head. Meanwhile Norbert wrote on the first scrap:

Sorry   Monty

'Yeah, well, never mind about that now. The important thing is to get that voice back before anything happens to it. Esme, you stay here. I'll pick you up later. Norbert come with me. We've got to sort this mess out.'

'Thanks a lot.' Esmerelda tutted and folded her arms. Monty kissed her on the cheek as he rose to leave.

'We won't be long, my dear.'

As they left the pub, Monty put an arm around Norbert's shoulder. His mood had softened.

'Just think, Norby,' he said with a smile, 'where would you be without me to look after you?'

Monty Banks and Norbert Quire made their way to Mrs Vox's house. They had the same difficulty Alfreda and Reg had had in finding the house. When they finally did so, Monty stood at the front door looking for the bell or knocker. Before he had a chance to find either however, the front door opened and there stood Mrs Vox.

'Hello, Mr Quire. I thought I recognised the sound of your footsteps at the top of the street. Come on in.'

Mrs Vox seemed to take no notice of Monty at all and in the hallway she spoke again to Norbert.

'Obviously *you* can't introduce your friend, so I suggest he does it himself.'

Only then did Mrs Vox acknowledge Monty's presence as she held out her hand to be shaken. Monty pushed himself forward and explained:

'I am Montgomery Banks, Mr Quire's close friend and business manager.'

'I see,' replied Mrs Vox, showing the two men into her sitting room.

'Now let me introduce my visitor. This is Alfreda Abbot.'

The two men turned to see a small girl sitting in one corner of the dark room with a dog at her feet. Norbert smiled at her as she rose from her chair and came over to present herself. She said no more than:

'Good afternoon, Gentlemen. Permit me to introduce my companion, Reginald.'

But in that moment Norbert's heart froze. His eyes opened

wide and his hands began to tremble, he could feel the hair on the back of his neck beginning to stand on end. His face drained of all colour. He looked as if he'd seen a ghost, or met himself coming in the opposite direction. As he felt his legs giving way underneath him, he staggered towards a chair.

'If you ask *me*,' said Alfreda, 'this young man is looking a trifle peaky.'

'It's probably a bit stuffy in here,' said Mrs Vox, and she went over to the large sash window and pulled it open. Norbert was thankful for the gust of fresh air that filled the room, and a stiff breeze began to play among the papers that lay around the room. Monty decided that enough time had been wasted with niceties and he wanted to get down to business.

'Mrs Vox, as Mr Quire's business manager, and as I have his best interests at heart, I am concerned that you have in your possession his voice. As you may or may not know, Mr Quire is a performer of great renown and his voice is very important to him because of that. I would therefore like to know what you intend to do with his voice.' Monty was very impressed by his little speech and thought it would more than likely intimidate this silly old bag into handing back the poet's voice. Mrs Vox, however, was not a woman to feel intimidated by anyone or anything.

'What I intend to do, Mr Banks, is to return the voice to its rightful owner.'

'What do you mean?'

'I mean that the voice I removed from Mr Quire yesterday belongs to Alfreda here.'

Monty looked with narrowed, suspicion-filled eyes at Joyce Vox. It was obvious that an evil thought was ripening in the darkness behind those eyes. The impresario replied slowly:

'I see.'

Then suddenly:

'So that's what you're up to. I get the picture. You steal my client's voice from him and give it to the midget here so that the pair of you can make a few bob and deprive this poor, innocent man of a decent living, taking the very bread from out of his mouth. I'll have the law on you. Both of you!'

Alfreda leapt to her feet and glared at Monty Banks. In a

booming voice full of anger and indignation, she said:

'**How dare you, sir! How dare you suggest that this good woman and myself are in league and involved in a criminal activity. That is a foul slur on *my* good name!**'

Monty looked at Alfreda, astonished at what he had heard. Then he turned to Mrs Vox and asked:

'What sort of a freak show did you get this little monster from? No wonder you want to change its voice! It ought to be locked up, or in a museum, I reckon.'

'Huh!' replied Alfreda. 'If anyone should be behind bars, it is *you*. *You*, sir are the villain of this piece. Never in all my born days have I come across such a black-hearted knave. You come into this house and dare to question the honour of this innocent woman! I have a good mind to knock you down, sir!'

And all this time, Norbert was sitting with his hands over his mouth hardly daring to breathe. He was listening to himself talk. It was *his* voice coming out of the little girl's mouth and, for the first time in his life, he was hearing himself speak. It made him cringe with embarrassment. He listened and squirmed. He had never heard anything so vain, pompous and self-important. And this was how he must have sounded to others for years! In that moment he made up his mind. He never wanted his old voice back again. He would do everything he could to keep the little girl's voice with its jokes and foolish stories and absurd poems and laughter. He didn't care what became of Alfreda, just so long as he didn't have to have that voice back. His heart began to harden in grim resolve.

Meanwhile, Monty Banks was beginning to lose patience with the Old Woman and the Midget. As a gust of wind swept in through the open window and stirred more and more papers, his mood became darker and more threatening.

'I've had enough of this messing around,' he said. 'I just want you to hand over Norbert's voice and then we can go home . . . and nobody needs to get hurt.'

'I hope you are not threatening the good Mrs Vox,' said Alfreda boldly. 'Because if you are, I should warn you that not only will you have *me* to answer to, but also Reginald here,

119

whose courage and ferocity are legend. He has been known to tear a man limb from limb!'

'Now hold on a minute,' said Reg, who felt that Alfreda was going a bit too far.

'That old fleabag couldn't tear up a piece of paper,' replied Monty with a sneer. Reg had to admit that Mr Banks was probably closer to the truth than Alfreda.

'Look, I don't want to get nasty about this,' said Monty. 'So give Mr Quire back his property and we won't bother you again, all right?'

He noticed that while he was talking, Mrs Vox shifted her position and was standing in front of the table with her hands behind her back, as if hiding something. Monty stepped forward and pushed her to one side. There, lying on the table, was a voice in a small plastic bag. He took the voice out of the bag and held it up to Norbert for him to have a look at.

'That the one?' he asked.

Norbert shrugged his shoulders. But as the two of them were inspecting it, Mrs Vox was standing quite still, breathing in deeply. She took more and more air down into her lungs, for a full thirty seconds. Then, as Monty was holding up the voice, she let all the air out in a great blast which ripped the voice from his grasp and sent it sailing out through the window. Once free and in the open air, the voice was picked up by the brisk afternoon breeze and set off dancing and floating down the street.

'That *is* the one!' shouted Monty. 'After it!'

In the same moment Alfreda realised what was happening and called to Reg:

'Up, Reginald, and at them! Your hour has come! CHAAAAARGE!'

Monty and Norbert made for the front door followed by Reg. Alfreda tried climbing out of the window but got stuck half way. From there she saw Monty and Norbert collide with each other by the garden gate and Reg took this opportunity to squeeeeeeeeeze underneath it. Once in the street he set off as fast as his legs could carry him in the direction of the wind-borne voice.

As Reg pounded down the road he kept the little voice in his sights all the time. It was wafted along high above him, kept aloft in the current of air. It fluttered and tumbled like a white butterfly, reckless and aimless, drifting and spinning round lamp-posts and trees. And then, at his back, Reg could hear the sound of heavy footsteps as Monty and Norbert came running down the street after him. Monty was weighed down by his large overcoat and Norbert followed close behind, his arms and legs flying in all directions like a mad wooden puppet. Now Reg could no longer tell whether the footsteps were getting closer or whether it was the sound of his heart thumping in his head as he flashed past parked cars and gateposts and pedestrians. But his legs were beginning to tire. He was finding it more difficult to catch his breath. He could feel himself slowing down, and all the time it seemed as if the footsteps were catching up with him. But he kept watching the floating voice high above him in the distance, chasing on after it, his tongue hanging out the side of his mouth like a little pink scarf.

The gusty afternoon breeze continued to play with the voice, puffing it this way and that, like a child with a bubble. Now it swooped down and waltzed with a paper bag, itself caught up in the wind's game. Now it soared upwards and continued its erratic flight down the road. It took to zigzagging, sending Reg back and forth across the road as he kept his eyes glued to it. Then suddenly it disappeared into a plane tree and Reg lost sight of it. He circled round the trunk of the tree at the bottom and looked up. He caught a glimpse of something gleaming white trapped in between some twigs. He looked back up the road and saw Norbert and Monty closing fast. They too had seen the voice disappear into the plane tree. There was no sign of Alfreda and all Reg could do was to hide and keep watch.

The panting old dog slipped underneath a nearby car and waited for Norbert and Monty to appear. Reg heard the sound of approaching footsteps, then Monty's voice:

'There it is. Up there! We need something to knock it down with.'

From his hiding place Reg could see the two men looking around for something to throw up at the voice to dislodge it from its resting place.

Norbert found a stout twig, broke it in half and gave half to Monty.

'Careful you don't break it,' said Monty as he sent his piece of wood spinning into the heart of the tree.

'Aren't you two just a little bit old to be throwing sticks at trees?' asked a passer-by out with her dog.

'Get lost!' replied Monty.

Reg, meanwhile, couldn't work out what had happened to Alfreda. Then he noticed Norbert dancing up and down on the spot and pointing frantically up the road. There was Alfreda, striding down the street and booming at the top of her voice:

'Ah ha! Caught you red-handed, you black-hearted villains! I will make you pay for your wickedness, just see if I don't!'

'Oh blimey! It's the midget,' said Monty as he sent his piece of wood winging toward the branch which held the gleaming white voice. This time he struck lucky and dislodged the voice. Monty let out a cry of triumph. Then he swore as he watched the voice drift down out of the tree and disappear behind a high fence. There was no way that Monty and Norbert could climb over the fence.

'We'll have to find a way round,' said Monty. 'Come on.'

Reg emerged from under the car just in time to stop Alfreda chasing after the two men. He explained what had happened and suggested that Alfreda lift him over the fence so that he could find the voice before Monty and Norbert got to it.

'Damn good plan, Reginald,' said Alfreda, and she heaved him up over the fence. At the top of the fence, Reg held on to the wooden paling with his front paws while Alfreda tottered around underneath him trying to support him. He surveyed the scene in front of him. It was a building site. Piles of earth lay around, alongside piles of bricks and broken planks of wood. To his left, Reg could see a man seated at an upturned wooden box which he was using as a table. He had been eating his lunch from off this box when, as if from nowhere, this funny-looking crisp had appeared next to his cheese sandwich. It was like it had fallen out of the sky. He picked it up and examined it, thinking it must be a new flavour. Then the man, who was a bricklayer by profession, noticed a dog looking over the fence. That's funny, he thought. That fence must be about seven foot tall. How come that dog's looking at me? He was still holding the funny-looking crisp in his hand thinking about the seven-foot dog, when it leapt over the fence, rushed over to him and bit him in the hand. The man let out a yelp and tossed away the 'crisp' as if *it* had bitten him. It landed some yards away on a pile of sawdust and Reg chased after it.

While the bricklayer was holding his injured hand, two breathless strangers came up to him. One of them, on the point of collapse from having run so far, gasped out:

'. . . . seen . . . . a dog . . . . come this way . .?'

The bricklayer pointed in the direction he had seen Reg disappear, and Monty and Norbert found him lying on top of the pile of sawdust, guarding Alfreda's voice. There was nothing else he could do. He couldn't pick it up in his mouth in case he swallowed it, and for once he was sorry he had paws instead of hands. He simply had to keep these two villains at bay until Alfreda arrived.

Monty and Norbert approached Reg slowly. One circled to the left of him, the other to the right.

'Good doggy, nice doggy. Let Uncle Monty have it!'

If there was one thing that Reg really hated it was being called 'doggy'. It made him very angry. As Monty bent forward to pick up the voice, Reg went for him snapping and barking. Monty leapt backwards in fright, and the two men continued circling cautiously around Reg waiting for their moment to pounce. Meanwhile the bricklayer appeared in order to find out what was going on. He saw the two men keeping a respectful distance from this dog that was snarling and growling and baring its teeth. This scene filled him with horror.

'Oh my God!' he said. 'It's got rabies!'

And he rushed off shouting for help and a doctor and an ambulance and the police. When Monty heard the word 'police' being shouted he looked at Norbert anxiously.

'I don't want to stick around here any longer than necessary. Let's get hold of this voice and scarper.'

With Norbert directly behind him and Monty directly in front, Reg didn't know which way to turn. Norbert grabbed him by the tail and tried to pull him away from the voice. Reg swung round and snapped at his attacker. At the same time Monty lunged forward and made a grab for the voice. But Reg was too quick for them. He swung back and snapped at Monty, who backed off fast. Reg was beginning to wonder how long he could hold out against these two. There was still no sign of Alfreda. Where was she?

Then Monty had an idea about how to deal with this pesky dog. He slipped his overcoat off his shoulders and approached Reg like a bullfighter with a cape. Reg swung round as Norbert tweeked his tail and the next thing he knew he was being enveloped in swirling blackness as Monty threw his coat over him, wrapped him up tight and rolled him over and over. Norbert picked up the voice from the ground and dancing up and down on the spot, showed it to Monty. He gave Reg a few more turns for luck, then said:

'Right, let's go!'

Alfreda arrived on the scene just too late to see the two villains hurry away from the building site. And as Reg was all bound up in Monty's overcoat, there was no way he could have known which way they went. Alfreda unravelled Reg and as he stood dazed, dizzy and exhausted, she shook him vigorously by the paw, saying in a deeply serious voice:

'Reginald, what words can express my admiration? Never, in the history of Human Conflict, has such Courage, and Loyalty, been shown by one, such as you! You are a Dog among Dogs!'

Reg was very touched by this little speech. In fact, it brought a lump to his throat.

Alfreda and Reg sloped back to Mrs Vox's house, disconsolate and dejected. By contrast, they found the old lady in a very jolly mood. She was humming a tune and tidying up the papers that the wind had scattered.

'How did you get on?' she asked.

'They got away with the voice,' replied Reg sadly.

'Good,' said Joyce.

Reg was taken aback by this, and Alfreda was infuriated:

'**Good!!?? Good!!??** How can you stand there and . .'

'If you just calm down for a moment,' said Mrs Vox, 'I'll explain. Firstly I shall give you your old voice back, Alfreda. Then we can sit and wait for Mr Quire. I'm sure he won't be long.'

Reg shook his head.

'I don't understand what's going on,' he said.

Chapter 17

'It must be really boring being right all the time, Mrs Vox,' said Alfreda, who had just looked through the curtains to see Norbert Quire standing anxiously by the front door. He had returned to the house he was hoping he'd never see again, and several times he'd decided he couldn't face Alfreda and the old lady. Finally, however, he realised he had no choice and rang the bell. Alfreda let him in.

' 'ello, Norbie. We've been waiting for you,' she said.

Norbert Quire, head bowed, shoulders hunched, entered the front room.

'Well, don't just stand there, Mr Quire. Spit it out. What do you want?' asked Joyce Vox.

'help-e-mer-gen-cy-a-lert-mrs-vox-i-can-not-func-tion-like-this-oth-er-hu-man-oids-think-i-have-blown-a-fuse-or-my-cir-cuits-have-gone-hay-wire-i-must-re-trieve-my-old-voice-help-e-mer-gen-cy-help-i-must-have-my-old-voice-back-a-lert-a-lert-a-lert . . .'

Alfreda and Reg just burst out laughing when they heard Norbert's robot voice.

'We'll have to call him The Norbot,' said Alfreda. 'Robert the Norbot!'

'You went chasing the wrong voice, didn't you, Mr Quire? Alfreda's was here all the time,' said Joyce.

'aff-irm-a-tive.'

'You can't tell the difference between your own voice and a robot's, can you?'

'neg-a-tive.'

Reg and Alfreda couldn't stop laughing, and in the end, even Norbert began to find it funny.

'har-har-har-har-har-har-har-har-har-har-har-har-har,' he laughed, mechanically.

Some time later, Norbert Quire was restored to his former self. It was unmistakeably the resonant, theatrical voice of old, but as he sat talking with Alfreda and Reg, it was clear that something had changed. It was gentler, calmer and more tranquil. Norbert Quire had learnt to listen and to laugh, and he was grateful to Alfreda for that. As he left the house, he admitted:

'I know I have been foolish, but I am not entirely sorry, simply because I have never enjoyed myself quite so much in my Life. And I hope we will all meet again soon.'

And with that he disappeared up the road, his walking stick clacking on the pavement and his coat billowing out behind him like a cloud.

'You two must be off too,' said Joyce Vox.

'Yeah, s'pose so,' Alfreda replied. 'I wonder what Mum and Dad'll say? It's funny, Mrs Vox, but with Norbot's voice I felt clever and strong and people didn't tell me to shut up and Dad was proud of me. I s'pose that'll all change.'

'Not necessarily,' replied the old lady. 'And anyway, there's not much point sounding clever with someone else's voice. Make your own voice stronger, and don't let people shut you up or shout you down.'

Reg and Alfreda left Mrs Vox, saying they would come and visit as often as possible because Reg wanted to listen to the other talking dogs on tape and Alfreda wanted to hear the praying pig and could Parkway come round because he likes maps, and could she bring Uncle Harry too? . . . .

On their way home Alfreda turned to Reg and said:

'I remember you saying you'd tell me about what happened on your day.'

'What's the point,' Reg replied. 'You'll only interrupt.'

'No I won't. Besides, you promised.'

'I'm sorry, but I'm not going to tell you about my day if I have to pause all the time when . . .'

'You don't have two paws, Reg. You've got four.' Alfreda burst out laughing. She thought this was the best joke anybody had cracked since . . . . well, since *she* cracked the best joke ever cracked.

'There you go!' said Reg. 'I haven't even started and already you've interrupted.'

'Okay, okay. I promise. I won't say a word. I'll just listen.'

Reg picked up his story from where he'd left off—his arrival at the railway station:

'I was met by this very smartly dressed woman who gave me an envelope and showed me to the train. She said I wasn't allowed to open the envelope until after the train had left, and that I had to eat the letter after I'd read it. Well, I had no idea where the train was going and as far as I could work out there wasn't another soul on it. It was all a bit spooky really. A whole train all to myself! Anyway, I read the letter in the envelope and at that point I realised I was going . . .'

But as Alfreda and Reg turned the corner at the top of the road where Mrs Vox lived, the sound of Reg's voice telling the story of his day was lost in the roar of passing traffic.

A Selected List of Fiction from Mammoth

While every effort is made to keep prices low, it is sometimes necessary to increase prices at short notice. Mammoth books reserve the right to show new retail prices on covers which may differ from those previously advertised in the text or elsewhere.

The prices shown below were correct at the time of going to press.

☐	416 24580 3	**The Hostage**	Anne Holm	£1.50
☐	416 96630 6	**A Box of Nothing**	Peter Dickinson	£1.75
☐	7497 0186 2	**The Granny Project**	Anne Fine	£1.99
☐	416 52260 2	**Sarah's Nest**	Harry Gilbert	£1.50
☐	416 51110 4	**Zed**	Rosemary Harris	£1.75
☐	416 54720 6	**Changing Times**	Tim Kennemore	£1.75
☐	7497 0344 X	**The Haunting**	Margaret Mahy	£1.99
☐	7497 0130 7	**Friend or Foe**	Michael Morpurgo	£1.99
☐	416 29600 9	**War Horse**	Michael Morpurgo	£1.75
☐	7497 0051 3	**My Friend Flicka**	Mary O'Hara	£2.99
☐	7497 0228 1	**The Vandal**	Ann Schlee	£1.99
☐	416 51880 X	**Journey of a Thousand Miles**	Ian Strachan	£1.75
☐	416 95510 X	**Ned Only**	Barbara Willard	£1.75
☐	416 62280 1	**Archer's Goon**	Diana Wynne Jones	£1.75
☐	416 22940 9	**The Homeward Bounders**	Diana Wynne Jones	£1.50

All these books are available at your bookshop or newsagent, or can be ordered direct from the publisher. Just tick the titles you want and fill in the form below.

Mammoth Books, Cash Sales Department, P.O. Box 11, Falmouth, Cornwall TR10 9EN.

Please send cheque or postal order, no currency, for purchaser price quoted and allow the following for postage and packing:

UK	55p for the first book, 22p for the second book and 14p for each additional book ordered to a maximum charge of £1.75.
BFPO and Eire	55p for the first book, 22p for the second book and 14p for each of the next seven books, thereafter 18p per book.
Overseas Customers	£1.00 for the first book plus 25p per copy for each additional book.

NAME (Block letters) ....

ADDRESS ....

....